Jane Withers

and the

Phantom Violin

An original story featuring
JANE WITHERS
famous motion picture star
as the heroine

By ROY J. SNELL
Illustrated by HENRY E. VALLELY

WILDSIDE PRESS

TABLE OF CONTENTS

ILLUSTRATIONS

ILLUSTRATIONS

"Jane! They Saw Me!" Jeanne Whispered

JANE WITHERS
and the
PHANTOM VIOLIN

CHAPTER ONE

THE SHIP'S GHOST

"Jane! They saw me!"

The little French girl, Petite Jeanne, sprang noiselessly through the cabin door. Then, as if to keep someone out, closed the door and propped herself against it. "They saw me!" she repeated in a whisper. "And they—I believe they thought me a ghost. I'm sure it was so. I heard one of them, he said 'ghost.' I heard him!" Jeanne clasped and unclasped her slender fingers.

"Who saw you?" Jane stared at her through the dim light of the moon that came straying through the narrow window.

"Yes. Who saw you?" came from somewhere above them.

"The men." Jeanne was growing calmer. "There were two of them. They saw me. They had tied their boat to the wreck. They were going to do something. I am sure of that. Then they saw me and acted very much afraid. And then—"

"You *do* look like a ghost," Jane broke in. "In

11

that white dressing gown with your golden hair flying in the moonlight, you look just like a ghost. And
I suppose you popped right up out of the hatch like
a ghost!" She laughed in spite of herself.

"But these men—" her tone sobered. "What were
they doing here at this time of the night?"

"That?" said Jeanne. "How is one to know? They
rattle chains. They see me, then Old Dizzy lets out
one of his terrible screams, and they are gone!"

Closing her eyes, the little French girl saw all that
had happened just as if it were being played before
her on a stage. She saw dark waters of night, a golden
moon, distant shores of an island, black and haunting and, strangest, most mysterious of all, the prow
of a great ship rearing itself far above the surface
of Lake Superior's waters.

The ship was a wreck—you would have said a
deserted wreck. And yet, even as you said it, you
might have felt the hair rise at the back of your neck,
for, appearing apparently through the solid deck, a
white apparition rose at the prow. Rising higher and
higher, it stood at last a wavering ghost-like figure
in that eery moonlight. This was her own figure
Jeanne was seeing now. Once again, with eyes closed,
she seemed to stand there in her wavy gown of filmy
white, bathed in the golden moonlight. Once again
she looked at the glory of the night, the moon, the
stars, the black waters, the distant, mysterious shores

where no one lived.

The distant shore line was that of Isle Royale fifteen miles off the shore of Canada, in Lake Superior.

All this was a grand and glorious dream to her.

They had been here three days, she and Jane Withers, and Greta Clara Bronson, whom she had known for but two months.

"Tomorrow," Jeanne had whispered to herself, standing there in the moonlight, "we are going ashore, ashore on that Mystic Isle."

Ashore? One would have said she must be standing on a ship lying at anchor. This was not true. The old *Pilgrim,* a three hundred foot pleasure boat, would never sail again. Fast on the rocks, her stern beneath the black waters, her prow high in air, she would rest there a while until—ah, well, until, who could say what or when?

"This," the little French girl had whispered, "is our summer home." How the thought had thrilled her! Three girls, the "last passengers," they had styled themselves, three girls alone on a great wrecked ship for long summer months.

What fun it had been to fit out the captain's and the first mate's cabin—what fun and what work! Bunks had been leveled, chairs and tables fitted with two short and two long legs to fit the slanting floors, a score of adjustments had been made. But now they were all done.

"And tomorrow," she had repeated in a whisper, "tomorrow—"

But what was that? Had she caught a sound? Yes, there it was again, like the purring of a cat, only louder. It came from the dark waters of night. Listening, intent, motionless, she had failed to fathom its meaning.

"Something on shore," she had tried to assure herself.

"Ashore." At once her keen young mind was busy conjuring up fantastic pictures of those shores which, though so near, scarcely a half mile away, were utterly strange to her. Wild moose, wandering about like cattle; wolves, tawny gray streaks in the forest; high ridges; great boulders laden with precious green stones; and in the silent waters of narrow bays such monstrous fish.

"Ah!" she breathed. "Tomorrow!"

But again her mind was caught and held by that strange sound, a very faint put-put-put.

Even as she listened the sound ceased. Then of a sudden she felt a thud that shook the wrecked ship. At the same instant she made out a dark bulk that was, she felt sure, some form of a craft.

"Men!" she thought with a shudder. "Men coming to the wreck in the night! I wonder why?"

She was frightened, dreadfully afraid. She wanted to escape, to drop through the hatchway, to go where her friends were in the cabin below. Her feet would not move. So there she stood, white-faced, tossing gold-white hair, waving white robe, a pale ghost in the moonlight.

What did the men on that boat think of her? Of course there were men, two of them, on the deck of that small, black power boat. For the moment they did not see her.

"Why are they here?" Jeanne asked herself. "What will they do?"

This indeed was a problem. The ship had been relieved of her cargo, all but a few barrels of oil in the hold that could not be easily reached. Even the brass fittings had been removed.

"There is nothing they could want," she assured herself, "absolutely nothing. And yet—"

Jeanne was gifted with a most vivid imagination. This old ship had sailed the seas for more than forty years. What unlawful deeds might not have been done within this grim old hull! There had been smuggling, no doubt of that. The ship had visited the ports of Canada a thousand times. What secret treasure might still be hidden within this hopeless hulk? She shuddered at the thought.

"All we want," she breathed, "is peace, peace and an opportunity to explore that beautiful island."

Strange to say, the little French girl was not the only person who at that moment felt a cold chill run up her spine. One of the men, the tall one on the little schooner, had caught sight of a patch of wavering white far up on the prow.

"Mart!" he was saying to his companion, and there was fear in his voice. "Do you think anyone ever died on this old ship?"

"Of course. Why not?" His companion's voice was gruff. "What do you think? She's sailed the lakes for forty years, this old 'Pilgrim' has, and why wouldn't people die on her, same as they die on other ships?"

"Then," the other man's words came with a little shudder, "then it was a lady that died, for look! Yonder in the prow is her ghost a-hoverin' still."

The other man looked at the swaying figure all in white, and he too began to sway. It seemed he might drop.

Seeming to collect his strength with great effort, he seized the line that held his own tiny craft to the wrecked ship, then grasping a pike pole, was prepared to give it a mighty shove that would send it far out.

At this very moment a strange and terrible sound smote the air; a wild scream, a shrill laugh, all in one it rent the still night air three times, then all was still.

· The man with the pike pole shuddered from head to foot. Then, regaining control of his senses, he gave a mighty heave that set his small craft quite free of the apparently haunted ship.

The boat had not gone far when a curious animate thing that seemed neither man nor beast burst from the narrow cabin. The thing began roaring and dancing about the deck like a baboon attacked by hornets. On the creature's shoulders was something four times the size of a man's head. The upright body was quite as strange as the head. As the boat continued its course the great round head rolled off and a smaller one appeared. This small head bobbed about and roared prodigiously, but all to no purpose. The little black boat had moved straight on to pass at last from sight into the night.

Then, and not until then, did the wisp of white, which, as you know, was Petite Jeanne, glide forward and vanish. She burst excitedly into a dark cabin.

"I heard chains rattle," Jeanne repeated, standing still in the cabin doorway. "One of the men spoke. They looked up at me. I wanted to run, but I couldn't. My—my feet wouldn't budge!"

She began dancing around the small cabin in her excitement.

"What happened then?" Jane demanded. "What did they do?"

"They—why, it was queer! They seemed in an awful hurry. They untied their boat and—

"Of course," she added as an afterthought, "there was Dizzy. He let out a most terrible scream, and laughed. How he did scream and laugh! Three times —one, two, three. They shoved off, those men did, as if their very life depended on getting away as fast as they could!"

"They thought you were a ghost," Jane chuckled. "Can't be any question about that. Who'd blame them? Look at you!"

"And then," Jeanne went on, "then some queer thing with two legs came out and danced wildly about the deck. He had an enormous head. By and by his head tumbled off, at least the awful big part, and I heard him roaring loud and angrily at the other men."

"Him?"

"Yes. It was a man in a diving rig. He'd taken off the helmet. Now, what do you think of that?"

Quite out of breath, the blonde-haired little French girl dropped down upon a berth at the side of the cabin.

"Man in a diving suit." Jane spoke in a matter-of-fact tone. "Going to dive, of course."

"But why?"

"That's right. Why?" Jane's brow wrinkled in thought.

"I wish—" she said slowly after a period of silence, "wish they hadn't come."

She was to wish this many times in the days that
were to follow. And then she was to change her
mind.

CHAPTER TWO

As Jane Withers and Jeanne sat there in the dark, whispering and wondering about the strange black schooner and its purpose in these waters, wondering too whether they dared light a candle and heat water for tea, something moved in the berth above their heads, and they became once more conscious of the third member of their party, Greta Clara Bronson.

It was because of this girl that the three friends were living in this old wreck off the shores of Isle Royale. Greta was slender, rather tall, with black hair, snapping black eyes, and a body that was a fine example of perpetual motion. She was recovering from an attack of hay fever and asthma. That is why she was here, why they were all here. Isle Royale is a rare retreat for hay fever victims.

Two months before, Jeanne had met Greta and had fallen in love with her. Greta could dance almost as well as Jeanne. She played the violin "divinely," as Jeanne expressed it. So when, one midsummer day, Jeanne found her friend sitting up in bed panting for breath, and was told that only a summer on Isle Royale could bring back to her the

joy of life, she had hurried away to find Jane. Together they had plotted and planned. And now, here
they were.

But why on a wrecked ship? Are there no hotels
on the island? Yes, there are hotels on Isle Royale.
But what trio of happy, energetic, adventure-loving
girls would choose a hotel rather than the deck of a
wrecked ship for a summer outing? Some might, but
not Jane, Greta, and Jeanne.

The only fear, expressed by them a half hour later
over their tea, was that some unforeseen event might
drive them from their strange retreat.

"Who's afraid?" Jane swung her arms wide. And
who indeed could be, with Jane as her protector?

Swen Petersen, a fine young fisherman, had let
them take a gun. "Not that you'll ever need one,"
he had told Jane. "All us fisher folk are simple and
honest. And you're not allowed to shoot animals on
the island. It's a game preserve. But you might feel
safer if you had my rifle to look at once in a while."
So he had left it.

Jane smiled as she recalled his words. She was
enjoying "looking at it" this very moment. More
than once she had taken it down to handle it lov-
ingly. Once, on seeing a bit of wood bobbing in the
water, she had taken aim and fired. The short, stout
rifle had a great roar to it. And Jane had a steady
aim; she had split the wood in two, first shot.

"All the same," she thought to herself, "I wish people would not prowl around the boat at night. And what would one dive for?" she asked herself. "Three or four barrels of oil in the hold—surely they are not worth all that trouble."

Then it struck her suddenly that here was a mystery and perhaps some great secret.

"Does this broken hulk of a ship hide some rich treasure?" she asked herself.

She laughed the thought down, but it bobbed up like a cork in water, more buoyant than ever.

"The ship's ghost is gone!" she exclaimed, springing up. "I wonder if those men will come back. I'm going to see."

"And leave us here?" Greta, too, was on her feet. Youngest of the trio, she was unaccustomed to wild, out-of-the-way places.

"Come along," Jane invited. "No ghost costumes though! Get into your long coats."

A moment later three dark shadows stole out upon the slanting deck of the wrecked ship.

"Boo!" Greta gripped Jane's arm. "How spooky it all is in the moonlight!"

"And just think!" Jeanne whispered. "Thousands of people have walked this deck, thousands upon thousands! The ship's more than forty years old. Thousands of those passengers will never walk any deck again. They are gone from this world forever."

"I Wish People Would Not Prowl Around at Night."

"Oh—oh! Jeanne, don't talk like that!" dark-eyed Greta implored.

"But where's your black schooner?" Jane demanded.

"Gone for good, I guess," Jeanne said after scanning the dark waters.

"For good?" Jane murmured. "I wonder."

For a full half hour they marched arm in arm up and down the broad deck. During all that time not a dozen words were spoken. It was a time for thought, not for speech. Here they were, three girls alone on the deck of a wrecked ship. They hoped to make it their summer home. Were intruders to bring all this to an end?

"Not if I can help it!" Jane told herself.

"Swen told us we would not be disturbed," she thought. "No one lives near. The Tobin's Harbor settlement is five miles away. Blake's Point with its rugged reefs and wild waves lies between. Few small craft pass that way.

"Oh well," she whispered to herself, "tomorrow we will row over to Duncan's Bay. Perhaps we'll find some trace of the black schooner there."

After that, for many long moments she gave herself over to contemplation of the scene of wild beauty that lay before her. The golden moon, dark waters, a shore line that was like a ghostly shadow, the wink and blink of a distant lighthouse, all this seemed a picture taken down from an art museum wall.

"Come!" she said at last, giving two slender arms a squeeze. "Come, we must go in. Tomorrow is another day."

CHAPTER THREE

A PHANTOM OF THE AIR

"It's a phantom, a phantom of the air!" Body aquiver, her black eyes reflecting the light of the setting sun, Greta stood intent, listening with all her attention.

A moment before, she had been hearing only the goodnight song and twitter of birds. Strange sounds they were to her. Bird songs all the same. But now this. "It is celestial music from heaven!" she whispered. Yet as she thought it, she knew that was not true. A musician herself, she had recognized at once the notes of a violin.

The sound came from afar. At times a light breeze carried it quite away.

"It may be miles away. In this still air sound carries far. But where can that one be who plays so divinely?"

To this question she could find no answer. She was standing on a narrow, natural platform of stone. Before her, almost straight down two hundred feet, were the black waters of Duncan's Bay. Miles away, with ridges, tangled jungles and deep ravines between, was the nearest settlement.

She had climbed all the way up Greenstone Ridge

from the shore of Duncan's Bay that she might be alone, that she might think. She was not thinking now. She was listening to such music as one is seldom privileged to hear.

Yes, she had climbed all that way through the bush that she might think. Greta was an only child. This was her first long journey away from home. Tears had stood in her mother's eyes as she bade her good-by, yet she had said bravely enough, "You must go, Greta. The doctor says you will escape the hay fever. I cannot come with you. You will be safe and happy with Jeanne and Jane. Good-by, and God bless you!"

There were times when this dark-eyed child recalled those words, when great waves of longing swept over her, when her shoulders drooped and all her body was aquiver. At such times as these she wanted nothing so much as to be alone.

As she had stepped into the still shadows of the evergreen forest at the back of the camping ground on Duncan's Bay that afternoon, she had been caught in such a wave of homesickness as would seem for the moment must sweep away her very soul.

"Jane!" she had called, and there was despair in her heart. "Jane, I am going to climb the ridge. You and Jeanne go on. I have my flashlight. I—I'll be back after the sun has set."

"All right," Jane had called cheerfully. "Don't go

over the ridge. If you do you'll get lost. Keep on this
side. If you lose your way, just come down to the
water's edge and call. We'll hear you and come for
you in the boat."

"Oh!" the slim black-eyed girl had breathed. "Oh,
how good it will be to be alone—to watch the sun
set over the black waters and to know that the same
sun is making long shadows in our own back yard at
home, and perhaps playing hide-and-seek in mother's hair!"

She turned her face toward the rocky ridge that
towered above her and whispered to herself once
more, "Alone, all alone."

Strangely enough, though no one is known to in-
habit Greenstone Ridge, and surely no one at that
hour would be found wandering there so far from
the regular haunts of men, she had experienced from
the first a feeling that on the ridge she was not
quite alone.

"And now," she breathed, "I know I am not alone
up here. There is someone else somewhere. But who
can that person be? And where?"

Here indeed was a mystery. For the moment
however, no mystery could hold her attention. Even
thoughts of mother and the sunset were forgotten.
It was enough to stand there, head bare, face all
alight, listening to that matchless melody.

As Jane had pushed her stout little boat off the

sandy shore that afternoon, she had been tempted to call Greta back. "Perhaps," she said to Jeanne, "we have made a mistake in allowing her to lose herself in that forest alone."

"But what can harm her?" Jeanne had reasoned. "Wolves are cowards. The wild moose will not come near her. There is no one on the ridge. It will do her good to be alone."

Thus reassured, Jane had straightened the line on her pole, hooked a lure to a bar on her reel, and, with Jeanne in the stern of the boat, had rowed away.

Someone had told Jane that the waters of Duncan's Bay were haunted by great dark fish with rows of teeth sharp as a shark's. From that time the girl had experienced a compelling desire to try her hand at catching these monsters. Now she breathed a sigh of suppressed excitement as she unwound a fathom of line from her reel.

"You do it this way," she said to Jeanne. Her whole being was filled with a sort of calm excitement. "An old neighbor told me how to fish for pike. You put this red-and-white spoon with its three-barbed hook on the line. Then you let the line out, almost all of it, a hundred and thirty feet. Then you row around in curves. You drag that red-and-white spoon after the boat. See?"

Jeanne nodded. "And—and what happens then?"

She had caught a little of the other girl's wild excitement.

"Why then of course the fish takes the whirling spoon."

"But what does he want with the spoon?" Jeanne's brow wrinkled.

"He thinks—" Jane hesitated, "well, maybe he thinks it's a herring or a perch. Perhaps red makes him mad. He's a wolf, this pike is, the wolf of all dark waters. He eats the other fish. He—but come on!" her voice changed. "Let's get going. It will be dark before long. You let out the line slowly while I row."

For some time after that, only the thump-thump of oars and the click of the reel disturbed the Sabbath-like stillness of that black bay, where the primeval forest meets the dark water at its banks and only wild creatures have their homes.

"There!" Jeanne breathed. "It's almost all out." She sat in the back seat and, lips parted, pulse throbbing, waited.

They circled the dark pool. The sun sank behind the fringe of evergreens. A bottle-green shadow fell across the waters. They circled it again. A giant dragonfly coursed through the sky. From afar came the shrill laugh of a loon. A deep sigh rose from nowhere to pass over the waters. A ripple coursed across the glassy surface. And then—

"Jane! Stop! We've hit something! The line! It's burning my fingers!" Jeanne was wild with excitement.

"Here! Give it to me!" Jane sprang up, all but overturning the boat. Gripping the rod, she reeled in frantically. "It's a fish!" Her words came short and quick. "I—I feel him flapping his tail. He—he's coming. Must have half the line. Here—here he comes. Two—two-thirds.

"Oh! Oh! There he goes!" The reel screamed. In her wild effort to regain control, Jane felt her knuckles bruised and barked, but she persisted. Not ten feet of line remained on the reel when the fish reluctantly halted in his wild flight.

"He—he's hooked fair!" she panted. "And the line is stout, stout as a cowboy's lariat. We—we'll get him! We'll get him!"

Once again she reeled in yard after yard of the stout line.

This time she fancied she caught a glimpse of a dark shadow in the water before a second mad rush all but tore rod and reel from her grasp.

"Jane! Let the old thing go!" Jeanne's tone was sober, almost pleading. "Think what a monster he must be! Might be a swordfish or—or even an alligator."

"This," said Jane, laughing grimly, "'is Michigan, not Florida. There are no alligators in Lake

Superior."

Once again she had the fish under control and was reeling in with a fierce and savage delight. "He's coming. Got to come. Now! Now! Now!"

CHAPTER FOUR

CAPTIVATING PHANTOM

The music to which Greta listened was unfamiliar. "Is it a song?" she whispered, "or an evening prayer? Who could have written it? Perhaps no one. It may have come direct from heaven."

She could not believe it. Someone was playing that violin. Real fingers touched those strings. She longed to search them out, to come before that mysterious person of great enchantment and whisper, "Teach me!"

Ah yes, but which way should she go? Already darkness was falling.

"No! No!" she cried as the music ended. "Don't stop! Go on, please go on!" It was as if the phantom violin were at her very side.

The music did not go on, at least not at once. Emerging from its spell as one wakes from a dream, she became once more conscious of the good-night song of birds, the dull put-put-put of a distant motor, the cold black rocks beneath her feet, the dark waters far below where some object, probably Jane and Jeanne in the boat, moved slowly forward.

And then her lips parted, her eyes shone, for the phantom had resumed his song of the strings.

In strange contrast to all this, Jane continued her battle with the big fish. In this struggle she was meeting with uncertain fortune. Now she had him, and now he was gone. She reeled in frantically, only to lose her grip on the reel and to see her catch disappear in a swirl of foam. At last, when her muscles ached from the strain, the fish appeared to give up and come in quite readily.

"There! There he is!" Jeanne all but fell from the boat when she caught one good look at the monster. He was fearsome beyond belief, a great head, two rows of gleaming teeth, a pair of round, glassy eyes. And, to complete the picture at that moment, over the bottle-green waters a long ripple ran like a long green serpent.

"Jane!" she screamed. "Let go! It's a snake! A forty-foot-long snake!" The slight little girl hid her eyes in her hands.

No need for this appeal. In a wild whirl of foam the thing was gone again. But still fastened to his bone-like jaw was the three-barbed hook. And the line, as Jane had said, was stout as a cowboy's lariat. She had him.

Strangely enough, at that moment one of those thoughts that come all uninvited, entered Jane's mind. "What did that diver on the black boat want on our wreck?"

No answer to this disturbing question entered her

Jane Reeled Her Line in Frantically

mind. They had left the ship unguarded. They had come to Duncan's Bay prepared to stay at least for the night. That they would stay she knew well, for the wind was rising again. To face those dark, turbulent waters at night would be perilous. "What may happen to the ship while we are gone?" she asked herself. Again, no answer.

The melody, faint, coming from afar, indistinct yet unbelievably beautiful, having reached Greta's ears once more and entered into her very soul, she stood as before, entranced, while the light faded. She was, however, thinking hard.

"Where can it be, that violin?" she whispered.

Where indeed? On that end of Isle Royale there are two small settlements. To reach the nearest one from that spot would require three hours of struggling through bushes, down precipices and over bogs. The traveler would be doing very well indeed if he did not completely lose his way in the bargain. It was unthinkable that any skilled violinist would undertake such a journey only that he might fling his glorious music to the empty air about Greenstone Ridge. It was even more unthinkable that anyone could have taken up his abode somewhere among the crags of that ridge. On Isle Royale there are summer homes only along the shore line, and there are very few of these. The three hundred and more square miles of the island are for the most part as wild and uninhabited as they must have been before the coming of Columbus.

"It is a phantom!" Greta whispered. "A phantom of the air, a phantom violin."

Had she willed it strongly enough, she might have gone racing away in fear. She did not will it. The music was too beautiful for that. It held her charmed.

What piece was it the mysterious one played? She did not know or care; enough that it was played. So she stood there drinking it in while twilight faded into night. Only once had she heard such music. In a crowded hall a young musician had stood up and, all unaccompanied, had played like that.

Could it be he? "No! No!" she murmured. "It cannot be. He is far, far away."

Then a thought all but fantastic entered her mind. "Perhaps I have radio-perfect ears." She had heard of people, read of them in some magazine, she believed, whose ears were so attuned to certain radio sounds that they could receive messages, listen to music with their unassisted ears.

"It has never been so before," she protested. "Yet I never before have been in a place of perfect peace and silence." The thought pleased her.

And then, as it had begun, the marvelous music died away into silence.

For ten minutes the girl stood motionless. Then, seeming to awake with a shudder to the darkness all about her, she snapped on her flashlight and went racing over the narrow moose trail leading away to the distant camping grounds of Duncan's Bay.

CHAPTER FIVE

The little drama, in which Jane and Jeanne played major roles, continued.

Duncan's Bay is primeval. Not an abandoned shack marks its shores, not a tree has been cut down. When darkness falls this bottle-green bay, reflecting the trees, shut in by the gloom of the forest, casts a spell over every soul who chooses to linger there.

It is a solitary spot. Six miles away, around a wind-blown, wave-washed point there are human habitations, none nearer. Little wonder, then, that the frail, blonde-haired Jeanne should renew her pleading.

"Jane, let that thing go!"

The "thing" of course was a living creature caught on Jane's hook at the end of the stout line.

"But Jeanne," Jane remonstrated, "I *can't* let him go!"

"Cut the line!" Jeanne was insistent.

"It cost two dollars. And that red-and-white spoon cost another dollar. Shall I throw three dollars into the lake?

"Besides," Jane began reeling in once more, "the thing's a fish, not a snake. There are no boa con-

39

strictors in America. He's just a big, old northern
pike. Looks like a snake, that's all.

"I—I'll bring him in," she panted. "You just take
a good look."

She reeled in fast. The fish, at last weary of battle,
came in without a struggle and, for one full moment
lay there upon the surface of the water. A magnificent specimen of his kind, he must have measured
close to four feet from tip to tail. His eyes and cruel
teeth gave him a savage look, but in that failing light
his sleek, mottled sides were truly beautiful.

"Wolf of the waters," Jane murmured. "Truly
you do not deserve to live! If a herring, gorgeous
flash of silver, passes your way, there is a mad swirl
and his favorite pool knows him no more. The beautiful speckled trout and the perch .fare no better.
Even little baby ducklings that sport about on the
surface are not safe from your cruel jaws. A swirl, a
frantic quack, qua-a-ack, and he is gone forever. And
yet," she mused, "who am I that I should set myself
up as a judge of wild life?"

"Jane," Jeanne pleaded, "let him go! What do
we want with him?"

"Why! Come to think of it, we couldn't really
make much use of him." Jane laughed a merry
laugh. "He must weigh twenty pounds."

"And if you put him in the boat he might bite
you," Jeanne argued.

"Or break a leg with his tail." Jane laughed once more.

She flipped the line. The red-and-white spoon shot to right and left. She did it again. The fish turned. A third time the spoon rattled. There was a swirl of white waters, then darkness closed in upon the spot where the fish had been.

"He—he's gone!" Jeanne gasped.

"Yes. I gave him his freedom." Jane lifted the red-and-white spoon from the water to send it rattling to the bottom of the boat. "But think of the picture he would have made! 'Pike caught by girl in Duncan's Bay on Isle Royale.' Can't you just see it?

"But after all," she mused as the darkness deepened, "I don't think so much of that kind of publicity. If we could only have our pictures taken with some innocent wild creature we have saved from destruction, how much better that would be."

There was about this last remark an element of prophecy. But unconscious of all this, Jane took up the oars and prepared for a moonlit row back to the camping grounds.

"Listen!" She suddenly held up a hand for silence.

Across the narrow bay there ran a whisper. Next moment the glassy surface was broken by ten million ripples. At the same time a cloud covered the moon, and the world went inky black.

Directing her course more by instinct than sight, Jane sent her boat gliding right to the bottle-necked entrance to the bay. Then the moon came out.

For some time they sat in their tiny craft and stared in amazement. Beyond the entrance to Duncan's Bay lies a mile of jagged, rock-walled shore line. Against this wall waves were now breaking. As the two girls watched, they saw white sheets of foam rise thirty feet in air to spray one section of rocky wall only to rush on and on out to sea until it ended in a final burst of fury far away.

"Well," Jane sighed, "we're here for the night, whether we like it or not. I wonder if Greta's back."

Greta was not back. As they grounded their boat on the sandy beach, no dancing sprite came to meet them. Jane cupped her hand for a loud "Whoo-hoo!"

"Whoo-hoo," came echoing back from the other shore. After that the woods and waters were still. Only the distant sound of rushing waters against rocky shores beat upon their ears.

"We'll build a rousing campfire," Jane said as she sprang ashore. "If she's lost her way she'll see the light."

A small, dead fir tree offered tinder. The scratch of a match, then the fire flamed high. Larger branches of poplar and mountain ash gave a steadier blaze. "She's sure to see that," Jane sighed as she settled down upon a log.

There was not long to wait. Greta had indeed caught sight of that bursting flame. She had not, however, been lost. Truth is, she had never been lost in her life. There are those who have the gift of location; they always know where they are. It was so with Greta.

"Girls! Oh, girls!" She came bursting through the bush. "The strangest thing! A violin! A phantom violin! I'm sure it was a phantom. Who else could be playing so divinely up there on that ridge at this hour of the night? Such music!" She drew in a long breath. "Such music you never heard!"

She began a wild dance about the fire that surely must have equaled any performance there in the brave days of long ago when only Indians came to pitch their tents on this narrow camping ground.

"Now," said Jane as a broad smile overspread her face, "tell us what really happened up there on the ridge."

Greta did tell them. With the light of the fire playing upon her animated features, she told her story so convincingly that even Jane was more than half convinced that Greenstone Ridge truly was haunted by the ghost of some violinist of enduring fame.

"And after that, one more strange thing," Greta went on. "I went racing headlong down the trail until I almost pitched myself into the antlers of a giant

moose who hadn't heard me coming. That frightened me. I went head first down the ridge to tumble
against a tree. When I picked myself up I was at the
top of one more rocky cliff.

"I stood there panting," she took in a long breath.
"I listened for the moose. They don't chase you, do
they?"

"Not often, I guess." Jane threw fresh fuel on the
fire.

"Well, this one didn't. But I was afraid he might.
So I waited and listened." Greta paused.

"It was dark by that time," she went on at last. "I
looked down where you should be, and saw nothing.
I looked back at the ridge. It sort of curves there,
and—" Again she took a long breath. "I saw a light
—a thin, pale green light. It seemed to hover on the
side of the ridge. I—it—it frightened me. At first it
seemed to move. 'It's coming this way!' I told myself.
And you'd better believe my heart danced.

"But it didn't move. Just hung there against the
rocks. So, pretty soon I climbed back up to the trail
and ran, fast as I dared.

"Now," she sighed, "what do you think of that?"

"I think," Jane chuckled, "you have been seeing
things!"

"And hearing them," Jeanne added.

"But you don't think—" Greta spoke in a sober
tone. "You don't think that music could have been

Greta Tumbled Down the Ridge

played on the radio? That my ears picked it up?"

"No," Jane replied at once. "I think that's nonsense."

But the little French girl was not sure. She had heard of such things. Why doubt them altogether? Besides, here was a beautiful, glorious mystery. What more could one ask?

"Greta, I envy you!" She threw her arms about the little musician. "You are the discoverer of a great mystery. But we shall unravel this mystery together, you and I. Is it not so? *Mais oui!* And Jane," she added, "our brave Jane, she shall protect us from all evil."

In the end Jane was to have a word or two to say about this. If there were mysteries to solve, she must play some more active part than merely that of policeman.

CHAPTER SIX

A STRANGE CATCH

In the meantime there were things to do. The boat must be dragged up and turned over, to afford them a shelter for the night. Balsam boughs must be gathered. These are nature's mattresses. Over these their blankets must be spread. This accomplished, they would think of supper.

Three pairs of eager hands accomplished all this in a surprisingly short time. Then, over a fire that had burned down to a bed of glowing coals, they brewed tea, toasted bread, broiled bacon, and in the end enjoyed a delicious feast.

After this, with a great log at their backs, they sat staring dreamily at the fire.

"It's so good to live," Jeanne murmured.

"Just to live," Jane echoed.

"And breathe," Greta added. "You can't know how it feels to take one long, deep breath of this glorious air, after you have struggled and struggled just for a tiny breath of life."

For some time after that they sat in silence. Jane was thinking of the wreck, wondering what might be happening to it in their absence. In her short sojourn there she had come to love the old *Pilgrim* that

47

would sail no more. She thought back to the happenings of the night before.

"A diver," she thought. "He came in search of something. I wonder what? Will I ever know?"

Jeanne's thoughts were on her early life in France. She could not remember her mother and father, but she could remember the kind man and woman who had taken her into their household as a small child and reared her as their daughter. She remembered the gardens of flowers and the beautiful old chateau where she had lived during her early childhood. Then the war came and with it the big guns that destroyed the chateau and killed her foster parents.

From there Jeanne's thoughts roved to the months she had spent in the Alps with an aunt. Strange circumstances had brought to the door of their isolated cottage a tame bear. The bear and Jeanne had become great friends. Then Jeanne's aunt had died, and Jeanne was left alone. A kind gypsy and his band passing by offered to take her and her bear with him. Jeanne followed them and for some time she lived the life of a roving gypsy. It was of this gypsy, Bihari, and his band that she thought now. What had happened to him since she had come to America? Where was her bear?

"Bihari," she thought. "I wonder where he and his gypsy band are tonight? How nice it would be if he would come to America. He has talked of it many

times. Perhaps he is here now." And so her thoughts
wandered before the glowing coals of the campfire.

As for Greta, she was hearing again the magic
music of the phantom violin. "Some day," she told
herself, "I shall see that violin and the hands that
created that entrancing melody."

"Do you know," Jane at last broke in upon these
reveries, "Swen is a fine boy. I wish we could help
him with that boat affair he told about."

"What boat affair?" Jeanne looked at her.

"Don't you remember? He said it would help the
whole island. There are many fishermen living all
around the island. A boat comes twice a week for
their fish. And the captain pays so very little for their
fish! In these hard times money is so scarce the fishermen are being obliged to stay on the island all
winter. And some of them have no opportunity to
send their children to school.

"Swen says they are trying to charter a boat so
they can carry their own fish to market. Not a big
boat, but large enough. They've got some money
pledged. But it is not enough. So there you are."

Swen was a fine young fisher boy whose nets were
set not far from the wrecked *Pilgrim*.

He had pointed out to them what a wonderful
summer home the wreck might become. For a very
little pay he had assisted them in fitting up their
rooms. He had rented them a boat and had thrown

in much equipment besides.

"He's a fine boy," Jane repeated. "When hard times came he was planning to enter college. Now—"

"Now if we only could help him!" Jeanne put in eagerly, "he might go!"

"They live in a lighthouse," Greta said, "he and his people do. He told me."

"How romantic!" Jeanne hugged her knees. "We should see him in his lighthouse tower."

"But most of all I wish we could help him," Jane said. "All we need—" she prodded the ground with a sharp stick. "All we need is a barrel of gold. Greta wants a fine music teacher. I'd love to travel. Swen wants a boat for his people. And you, Jeanne, what is it you want?"

"I?" Jeanne laughed. "Only happiness for all my good friends."

"'A barrel of gold," Jane repeated dreamily. "And perhaps it is right beneath us, in this very soil."

"Beneath us?" Greta stared.

"Why not? A very small barrel, even a tiny keg. This spot, the only level ground on the shores of this bay, has been a camping ground for countless generations. The Indians came to Isle Royale to pound out native copper from the rocks. They built their campfires right here. Swen says if you dig down you will find the remains of those campfires still."

"How thrilling!" Greta's eyes were large with

wonder. "Suppose we dug down and found some treasure—a barrel of—. But then, Indians didn't have barrels, not even kegs." Her dream faded.

"The voyageurs did," Jane encouraged.

"Who were they?"

"The traders who came after the Indians. They camped here on their way across the lake. Can't you see them?" With outstretched hands, the girl stared into the darkness that is Duncan's Bay at night. "Great, stalwart men, muscles like iron bands, faces browned by the sun, eyes ever looking forward to fresh fields of adventure, the voyageurs!

"Perhaps—" her voice dropped to a low note of mystery, "perhaps they camped here one night with a great bag of gold. Perhaps they were expecting an attack by Indians and, thrusting their gold in their water barrel, buried it here, never to return."

"Yes," Jeanne smiled doubtfully, "perhaps they did. Anyway, you are right on one score. It's a barrel of gold we need."

"Just now," Jane laughed, "what we need most is a good night's sleep."

They went reluctantly to their balsam-scented bed.

Greta and Jeanne were weary. After listening for a time to the constant rush of water against the rocky shores of Blake's Point and staring at the ribs of their boat just over their heads, they fell asleep.

Jane did not fare so well. Lying there in that narrow bed beneath their boat, she found her mind going over the events of the day and of those days that had gone before.

She had always lived in the city but had loved the out-of-doors. She had often dreamed of the life of her pioneer ancestors and had wished she might have lived at that time. Life here on Isle Royale was as near the life of the pioneers as she had ever experienced. Her adventure with the huge pike had given her the feeling of having fought for and won her daily food. Just who had camped here before them? Why had they come? Why had they gone? And where had they gone? It would be fun to live the way the people of long ago lived—at least for a while. But would it be fun for long? These thoughts and many others floated through Jane's mind as she lay there half asleep and half awake, in her camp bed on the shore of Lake Superior.

Suddenly she sat up straight. The stretch of level land on which they were camped was hardly a hundred feet wide. Back of that was a sloping hillside where the spruce, balsam, and pine of a primeval forest battled for a place in the sun. From this forest she had caught some faint sound, the snap of a twig, the click of some hard object against a stone.

"It could be men," she whispered. "Just over that ridge is Tobin's Harbor. Many people live there.

But such a trail! Straight up! And on such a night. They—"

There it was again. She clenched her hands hard to prevent crying out. A loud click had sounded out in the night. "Like the raising of a rifle's hammer," she told herself.

But was it a rifle? She must see. Lying flat down, she pushed the covers quietly aside, rolled over twice and found herself beneath the dark night sky.

The moon was still shining. Her eyes soon accustomed themselves to the light. Still lying flat on the damp earth, she listened intently. What she heard set her blood racing. "Footsteps," she whispered, "in the night."

They seemed very near, those footsteps. But were they human footsteps? She doubted it. And from this came a sense of relief.

Raising herself on one elbow she peered into the night. At that moment a loud groan sent the chills down her spine.

The next instant she was ready to laugh. A giant old patriarch of his tribe, a moose with wide-spreading antlers had stepped out into the moonlight.

"A moose," she whispered. "Swen says there are a thousand or more on the island, and that they are harmless. But how old and feeble this one seems!"

She had judged correctly. The moose was nearing the end of his days. His giant antlers were a burden.

He walked very slowly and with many a groan. On the island he was known as Old Uncle Ned.

The girl's lips were parted in a smile when, of a sudden, the blood seemed to freeze in her veins. A second creature had appeared at the edge of the forest—a great, gaunt wolf.

At this instant, with one more groan, Old Uncle Ned stepped into the water and prepared to swim across the bay.

The bit of wild life drama witnessed by the girl during the next moment will never leave her memory. Neither the moose nor the wolf had seen her. The moose, no doubt, smelled fresh water grass on the other side. The wolf was eager for a kill.

Waiting in the shadows, the killer opened his mouth to show his white teeth, his lolling tongue. But the instant the aged moose was well in the water and, for the time, quite defenseless, with one wild spring his pursuer was after him.

"He—he'll kill that moose!"

Scarcely knowing what she did, in her excitement Jane sprang to her feet, seized the steel casting rod and, racing to the bank, sent the red-and-white spoon darting toward the swimming wolf.

The first cast fell short. The reel sang and she rolled in for a second try. All this she had done under the impulse of the moment, without planning.

Next instant she was awake to reality, for on a

The Gaunt Wolf Followed the Great Moose

second cast the spoon, striking the wolf on the back, slid down to at last entangle the three-pronged hook in the tangled hair of his bushy tail.

"Jeanne! Greta!" the girl screamed. "Wake up! I've caught a wolf!"

"Wake up yourself," Jeanne replied dreamily. "You are walking in your sleep. You let that fish go free long ago."

"No! No!" Jane, quite beside herself, protested. "Get up! Quick! Quick! I've caught a wolf. A real wolf of the forest!"

At the same time she was saying to herself, "Whatever am I to do?"

CHAPTER SEVEN

THE LAST PASSENGERS

Jane had the wolf by the tail, there could be no doubt about that. The three-pronged hook of her trolling spoon was securely entangled in that bushy mat of hair. The line that held the spoon was strong. What was she to do next?

The aged moose, awakened to his peril by the sound of her voice, threw his head about, took one startled look, then grunting prodigiously, went swimming for the other shore.

Turning angrily, the wolf began snapping at the hook. "Won't do to let him take more line," the girl told herself. "Got to give the poor old moose a chance."

At that moment Greta rolled from beneath the boat, leaped to her feet to stand staring, wild-eyed, at the scene before her.

"Jane! It's a wolf!" she cried.

"Yes, and I've got him!" Jane laughed in spite of herself.

"Let—let him go! Throw down the rod! Let him go!" Jeanne cried as she came tumbling out from her bed.

But Jane held tight. When the wolf turned about

to snap at the line, she reeled in. When he started away, he gave him line, but not too much. There was the venerable moose to consider. Having started the affair, she was determined to finish it.

"Let him go!" Jeanne's voice dropped to a terrified whisper. "Can't you see he's turning? He—he's coming this way. He'll eat us!"

Then, calmed by her sense of danger, she rushed back to the half burned out campfire, seized two smouldering sticks and waved them to a red glow. Rushing forward, she threw one at the gray beast who was swimming toward the camping ground.

The flaming stick struck the water with a vicious sizzle. Black on the instant, it nevertheless left its imprint on the wolf's brain. Once again he wheeled about.

The moose by this time had climbed up the opposite bank and disappeared, as much as to say, "Well, you go ahead and fight it out."

Strange to say, Jane at this moment began losing her calm assurance. She reeled in when perhaps she should have given line. It was astonishing the way the wolf came in. He had not half the pull of the great fish.

Before she knew it, his feet were on a sandbar. After that it was quite another story. He was not looking for a fight, that wolf. He was looking only for safety. With a mad dash he was down the sandbar, up the bank and into the forest.

Completely unnerved at last, Jane lost all control of the reel. After spinning round and round like mad, it came to a jerking halt. For one split second there was a tremendous strain on the line, then it fell limp.

"He—he's gone!" Jeanne breathed. "Broke the line."

"Maybe he did. I'm going to see." To her companions' utter consternation, Jane followed the wolf into the dark forest.

She returned some moments later. In her hand was the red-and-white spoon.

"Went round a tree and tore the hook out of his tail," she explained calmly. "See! Some gray hairs!" She held it out for inspection. "Gray hairs that's all I get. But the moose got his life back, for a time at least. Perhaps he's learned his lesson and won't try swimming bays again.

"You see," she explained, throwing some bits of birch bark on the fire and fanning them into a blaze, "a moose is practically powerless in deep water. If you catch up with him when you're in a canoe, you could leap into the water, climb on his back, and have a ride. He can't hurt you. But on land—that's a different matter."

When the excitement of the night had passed and everything was peaceful once more, Jeanne and

Greta crept back among their blankets and were soon asleep.

Jane remained outside. The wind had dropped, but still the rush of waves might be heard on the distant shore. This wild throbbing made her restless. She thought of the wreck. How was it standing the storm? Well enough, she was sure of that. But other more terrible storms? Her brow wrinkled.

"We could camp here," she told herself. "Get a tent or have some one build us a rough cabin. We could stay all summer. But then—"

Already she had begun to love their life on the wreck.

"It's different!" she thought. "Different! And that's what I want, things that are different, experiences that are different, a whole life that is different from any other."

"Well," she laughed a low laugh, "looks as if we were going to get just that, whether we stay on the wreck or on land."

Her thoughts were now on the mysterious black schooner that had visited the wreck the night before, and now on Greta's phantom violin and the strange green light.

"It may never happen again," she murmured. "For all that, Greta will go back again and again, when it is quite dark. People are like that."

She had turned about and was considering a re-

"We Could Stay Here All Summer," Jane Thought

turn to her nest beneath the boat when, of a sudden, she dropped on her knees in the dark shadows of a willow.

"There is something moving," she told herself, "moving out there in the channel."

At first she thought it a swimming moose, and laughed at her own sudden shock. Not for long, for as the thing came into clearer view she saw it was a power boat.

Moving along, it glided past her, dark, silent, mysterious in the night.

"The black schooner!" she whispered. "Wonder if it's been to the wreck!" Her heart sank.

"But no," came as an afterthought. "It has been too stormy. They are putting in here for the rest of the night."

When the schooner had passed on quite out of sight, she made her way to the overturned boat, crept beneath it and had soon found herself a cozy spot among the blankets. She did not fall asleep at once, but in time the silence put her to sleep.

When she awoke there was the odor of coffee and bacon in the air. Greta and Jeanne were getting breakfast.

"Boats leave no trails," she assured herself. "Unless they have seen the black schooner, I will not tell them it passed in the night."

A bright glitter was on the surface of the bay.

Old Lake Superior had put on a bland and smiling face. No trace now of last night's boisterous roaring.

"We'll get back to the 'Pilgrim' as soon as breakfast is over," Jane decided.

"But the barrel of gold?" Greta protested. "Aren't we going to dig for that?"

"No gold digging today," Jane laughed. "We have no spade. But you'll see! There's another day coming. We'll find it, don't you ever doubt it, a whole barrel of gold!"

Breakfast over, Jane and the girls gathered up their camping equipment and packed it away in the boat. Jane took the oars and sent their light craft skimming through the narrows and out into the broad stretch of water lying between Blake's Point and the reef that was the *Pilgrim's* last resting place.

"Look how he smiles!" she cried, throwing back her head. "Old Superior, the great deceiver! You can't trust him!"

And indeed you cannot. When a storm comes sweeping in over those miles of black waters and the foghorn on Passage Island adds its hoarse voice to the tumult of the waves, it is a terrible thing to hear those waves come roaring in.

Jane had accepted the judgment of old-time fishermen that for the time the wreck was a safe place to be. But this morning her brow wrinkled. "What if it should be carried out to sea!" she thought with a shudder. "And we, the last passengers, should be on board?" She said never a word to her companions who, reflecting the smile of Old Superior, were deliriously happy.

CHAPTER EIGHT

DIZZY'S WELCOME

As they neared the wreck, from somewhere inside it came one wild scream, then the maddest laugh one might ever hope to hear. Just such a laugh as on that other night had completed the task of turning Jeanne into a ghost and frightening the mysterious men of the black schooner away.

Had some stranger been present, he might have expected at this moment to see Jane drop her oars in surprise and consternation. Instead, she rowed calmly on, chuckling meanwhile.

"Dizzy's welcome!" she exclaimed.

"Good old Dizzy!" Jeanne chimed in.

Dizzy, as they had named him, had been aboard-ship when they arrived. At least they had found him swimming frantically about in the one-time dining room of the ship. He was a large loon. Crippled by some accident so he could not fly, he had somehow got into this place, but had failed to find his way out.

Almost starved, he had appeared to welcome their arrival. They had brought fresh trout and fed him. From this time on, with no apparent desire to leave the place, he had become a devoted pet.

"We'll be joining you shortly," Jane cried out to him as the boat bumped the side of the ship. This news was answered by one more delirious burst of mirth.

"One could almost think he was human!" Greta shuddered in spite of herself. For her this old ship had a haunting appearance.

Old Superior is ever ready enough to display his various moods. The girls had not been aboard an hour when a dense fog came sweeping in from the north.

"We could never find our way if we were out there now," Jane said with a shrug.

There came a slow, drizzling rain, followed by more and denser fog.

Two hours later a wild storm came sweeping in. Sheets of water, seeming at times to leap from the very lake, dashed against narrow cabin windows. There was a ceaseless wash-wash of waves against the black hull of the wreck. What did this mean to the happy trio? Nothing at all. They were down in their private swimming pool with Dizzy. Such a strange and wonderful swimming pool as it was too! Once the dining saloon of the great ship, it now lacked both chairs and tables, but the decorative railing leading to the floor above made a perfect diving board. A second rail ran slantwise into the water that at the far end must be twenty feet in depth.

"Shoot the shoots!" Greta cried as, sitting astride the rail, she shot downward to hit the water with a splash and to go swimming away. How Dizzy beat the water with his wings and screamed! How they laughed and splashed him! How he dove and swam!

"It—it's wonderful!" Jeanne bubbled, her mouth half filled with water. "And to think," she exclaimed as she dragged herself to a place beside Jane on the topmost step of the broad stairway, "to think that only a short time back all this was swarming with people off on a holiday! Some gay, some solemn, some rich, some poor, but all promenading the deck and all coming in here for their dinner. And now look! Here we are, only three. And it is all ours! And look at the cabins! Rows of them on either side, high and dry, half of them. People could sleep in them."

"But they never will," Jane said soberly. "We are the old ship's last passengers, no doubt about that. Next winter ice will form on the bay. Then a storm will come roaring in and break it all up. The ice will come tearing at the old ship and cut her in pieces, if she lasts that long." Jane had not meant to add this last bit; it just came out.

"Of course the ship will last the summer through." There was the slightest tremor in Jeanne's voice. "Everyone says that. S-o-o-o!" she cried in her old merry way. "Let us enjoy it all while we may!" Once again she sat astride the rail to go sliding down and lose herself in a mass of foam.

"Old ships," Jane thought, "are like old houses. They have secrets to tell. What stories the doors to those cabins could relate!" Her eyes swept the long array of cabin doors.

"But old ships as well as old houses keep their secrets well," Jane continued. "Often the stories of their treasures are entirely forgotten or become simply another tale of the sea—heard and soon forgotten. But enough of this dreaming." Jane jumped to her feet and the other girls, startled from their own day dreams, looked questioningly toward her.

They had set up a small stove in the captain's cabin. Five minutes later they were all three doing a wild Indian dance round the fire. This ended by a pow-wow in blankets, then a feast of smoked trout, hard crackers and some hot drink only Jeanne knew how to make. And still, outside, the wind drove rain against the windowpanes.

"If she lasts that long," Jeanne whispered under her breath. She was thinking of Jane's words about the ship.

For the time it appeared there was nothing to fear. The wind dropped at sunset. Clouds went scudding away and the moon, shining like a newly-polished copper kettle, hung over all.

After Greta and Jeanne had crept into their berths, Jane slipped into slacks and jacket to climb

They Did an Indian War Dance Around the Stove

the steps leading to the bridge. There, while the
moon sank lower and lower, she paced slowly back
and forth.

In common with all other girls, this girl had her
dreams. Strange dreams they were that night. For
her the ship was not a wreck, but a living ship riding
on an even keel, plowing its way through the dark
night waters. She was the captain on the bridge.
From time to time, as if for a word with the wheel-
man, she paused in her march; at times, too, appeared to jangle a bell. For the most part she paced
slowly back and forth.

"Why not?" she murmured at last. "Why should I
not some day command a ship? There would be
things to learn. I could master them as well as any
man, I am sure."

She paused for a moment's reflection. Had there
been other lady captains? Yes, she had read stories
of one who commanded a tugboat in Puget Sound.

And there had been the lady of the "Christmas
Tree Ship." The husband of this Christmas tree lady
had been lost on his craft while bringing thousands
of Christmas trees to Chicago. She had chartered
another ship and had carried on his work.

"What a glorious task!" the girl murmured.
"Bringing Christmas trees to the people of a great
city!

"She's dead now," she recollected. "That lady captain is dead. The Christmas tree ship sails no more. But it shall sail. Some day I shall be its captain. And Christmas trees shall be free to all those who are poor."

Laughing low, she once more resumed her walk on the bridge. This time her thoughts dwelt upon things very near at hand. "This wreck," she was thinking, "this old 'Pilgrim'—is it a safe place to be?

"It—it just has to be!" she exclaimed after a moment's reflection. "It's such a grand place for the summer. Broad deck, sloping a little, but not too terribly much. Cabins without number, a swimming pool that once was a dining hall. Who could ask for more? And yet—" her brow wrinkled. The little breezes that blew across the water seemed to whisper to her of danger.

At last, shaking herself free from all those thoughts, she went down to her cabin and was soon fast asleep.

CHAPTER NINE

The following day was bright and clear. The waters of Old Superior were as blue as the sky. Even the wreck took on a scrubbed and smiling appearance.

"It is as though we were all prepared to shove off for one more voyage," Jeanne said with a merry laugh.

As soon as the sun had dried the deck, Jeanne and Greta spread blankets and, stretching themselves out like lazy cats, prepared for a glorious sun bath.

It was a drowsy, dreamy day. In the distance a dark spot against the skyline was Passage Island where on stormy nights a searchlight, a hoarse-hooting foghorn, and a whispering radio warned ships of danger.

All manner of ships pass between Isle Royale and Passage Island. They were passing now, slowly and, Jeanne thought, almost mournfully. First came a dark old freighter with cabins fore and aft, then a tugboat towing a flat scow with a tall derrick upon it, and after these, all painted white and with many flags flying, an excursion boat. And then, reared over on one side and scooting along before the wind, a sailboat.

Just to lie in the sun and watch this procession was life enough for Jeanne and Greta, but not for Jane. She was for action. Dizzy needed fish. She would row over to the shoals by Blake's Point. There she would troll for trout.

The water about Blake's Point is never still. It is as if some great green serpent of the sea lies stretched among the rocks and keeps it in perpetual motion by waving his tail. It was not still when Jane arrived.

"Just right," she whispered, as if afraid the fishes might hear. "Rough enough for a little excitement, and no real danger."

Casting a shining lure into the water, she watched the line play out as she rowed.

A big wave lifted her high. Still the line played out. The boat sank low. She checked the line. Then, watching the rocks that she might not come too close and snag them, she rowed away.

For some time she circled out along the shoals, then back again. She had begun to believe there were no fish, and was musing on other things—phantom violins, black schooners, gray wolves, Old Uncle Ned—when, with a suddenness that was startling, her reel began to sing.

Dropping her oars, she seized the pole and began reeling in rapidly. Next moment she tossed a fine three pound trout into her boat. "You get 'em quick or not at all," Swen had said to her. She had got this one "quick."

An hour later four fine trout lay in the stern of her boat. "Enough," she breathed. "We eat tonight, and so does Dizzy."

The day was still young. She had not meant to visit Duncan's Bay, but now the place called to her.

Swen's short, powerful rifle lay in the prow of her boat. Why had she brought it? Perhaps she could not tell. Now she was glad it was there.

"I'll go ashore on Duncan's Bay," she told herself. "Go hunting phantoms and, perhaps, a gray wolf or two."

It was a strange wolf she was to come upon in the forest that day.

With corduroy slacks, stout shoes, a flannel shirt open wide at the neck, and a small hat crammed well down on her head, Jane might have been taken for a man as, rifle under arm, she trudged through the deep shadows of the evergreen forest covering the slope of Greenstone Ridge. The soft bed of needles cushioned her tread and she walked almost noiselessly along the narrow path.

That she was in her element was shown by the spring in her footstep, the glad, eager look in her eyes.

" 'I love life!' " She hummed the words of a song she had heard.

At times through a narrow opening she caught a

glimpse of gray gulls soaring like phantom ships over the water. To her ears came the long, low whistle of some strange bird. She was not surprised when she found herself standing face to face with a magnificent broad-antlered moose. She stood quite still.

Great-eyed, the moose stared at her. A sound to her right caught her attention. She looked away for an instant. When her gaze returned to the spot where the monarch of the forest had stood, he had vanished.

"Gone!" she exclaimed low. "He was taller than a man, yet he vanished without a sound! How strange! How sort of wonderful! But I wonder—"

But there was that sound from below. Snapping of twigs and swishing of branches. No moose that. She would see what was down there.

She did see, and that almost at once. A few silent steps, and she came upon him—a man. He was standing at a spot where a break in the evergreens left a view of Duncan's Bay.

He was looking straight ahead. On his face was a savage, hungry look. Only the night before the girl had seen that same look in the eyes of a wolf.

She was not long in learning the reason. In plain view through that narrow gap was the patriarch of his tribe, the moose she had saved from the wolf.

"But why that look?" She was puzzled, but not for long. In the hands of that man was a rifle. An ugly smile overspread his face. He lifted the rifle and took deliberate aim at the moose.

She recalled Swen's words: "Isle Royale is a game preserve. You will not be allowed to kill even a rabbit."

"This man is a poacher." Her mind, always keen, worked quickly. "I know I can save the moose, and I will!"

Swinging her own rifle into position, she fired well over the heads of man and moose. The shot rang out. The startled moose fled.

And the man? She did not pause to see. Like a startled rabbit she went dodging and gliding back and forth among the evergreens. In her mind, repeated over and over, was the question, "Did he see me? Did he see me?"

In the meantime the two girls on the wreck had been enjoying their sun bath and a sort of picnic lunch served on deck. Jeanne and Greta sat for a long time staring dreamily at the sea. Then Jeanne stood up, slim and straight and graceful on the planked deck.

"Wonder if I can have forgotten," she murmured. Then, seizing a tambourine, she began a slow, gliding and weaving motion that, like some beautiful work evolved from nothing by the painter's skillful hand, became a complicated, fantastic and wonderful dance.

Jane Swung Her Own Rifle into Position

For a full quarter hour Greta sat spellbound. She had seen dancing, but none like this. Now the tambourine was rattling and whirling over the little French girl's head, and now it lay soundless on the deck. Now the dancer whirled so fast she was but a gleam of white and gold. And now her arms moved so slowly, her body turned so little, she might have seemed asleep.

"Bravo! Bravo!" cried Greta. "That was marvelous! Where did you learn it?"

"The gypsies taught me." Dropping upon the deck, Jeanne rolled herself in a blanket like a mummy.

"People," she said slowly, "believe that all gypsies are bad. That is not so. One of the very great preachers was a gypsy—not a converted gypsy—just a gypsy.

"Bihari and his wife were my foster parents in France. They were wandering gypsies, but such wonderful people! They took me when I had no home. They gave me shelter. I learned to dance with my bear, such a wonderful bear. I wonder where he is now and if he still dances. I wish they were all here!"

Next moment she went rolling over and over on the deck. Springing like a beautiful butterfly from a cocoon, she whirled away in one more spritely, riotous dance.

It was in the midst of this that a strange thing happened. Music came to them from across the waters—wild, delirious music.

Jeanne paused in her wild dance. For a space of seconds she stood there drinking in that wild glory of sound.

Then, as if caught by some spell, she began once more to dance. And her dance, as Greta expressed it later, was "like the dance of the angels."

"Greta," Jeanne whispered hoarsely when at last the music ceased and she threw herself panting on the deck, "that is gypsy music! No others can make music like that. There is a boatload of gypsies out there by Duncan's Bay."

"Yes, yes!" Greta sprang to her feet. "See! It is a white boat. It is just about to enter the Narrows. Perhaps Jane will see it."

"Jane—" There was a note of pain in Jeanne's voice. "Jane has the boat. I cannot go to them. Perhaps I shall not see them—my friends, the gypsies. And they make music, such divine music!"

"Music—divine music," Greta thought with sudden shock. "Can one of these have been my phantom violinist?

"No," she decided after a moment's contemplation, "that was different. None of these could have played like that."

"It is the call!" Jeanne cried, springing to her feet

and stretching her arms toward the distant shore. Fainter, more indistinct now the music reached their ears. "The gypsies' call! I have no boat. I cannot go to see them."

CHAPTER TEN

SILENT BATTLE

Ten minutes of running and dodging brought Jane, still gripping her rifle, squarely against a towering wall of rock.

"Did he see me?" she asked herself. "And if he did?"

Dropping back into the protecting branches of a black old fir tree, she stood breathing hard, listening.

Her mind was in a whirl. She had saved the moose. But what of herself?

"It was probably a foolish thing to do," she muttered low. "And yet—"

Her mind took another turn. Who was this man? Certainly he was breaking the law. No man had a right to kill a moose on Isle Royale.

"They are one of the great joys of the island," she told herself. "Hundreds of people come just to see them. Nowhere else can one see them so easily and safely in their native haunts. If men begin to shoot them they will go to the heart of the island and no one will see them. What a pity!"

Again, who was this man? She thought of the black schooner that had come creeping up the bay in the dead of night and that other one Jeanne had seen by

the wrecked ship. Were they the same? And did this
man belong to that schooner? To none of these questions could she form a positive answer.

When she had rested there in the shadows until
she was sure the man had not followed her, she went
gliding along beneath the rocky ridge, then started,
slipping and sliding downward, to the camping
ground.

Like a patient steed her boat lay waiting on the
beach.

"Should hurry back to the ship," she told herself.
But the waters of Duncan's Bay, so peaceful, so un-
disturbed and deserted, seemed to call. She answered
that call.

After rowing quietly for a half hour, she dropped
her oars, took up her rod and began to cast. Her reel
sang, the spoon gave off a silvery gleam as, cutting
a narrow arc through the air, it sank from sight.

Without truly hoping to catch a fish, she reeled in
slowly. She repeated this again and again. Her boat
was drifting. She gave no attention to that. Each cast
was straighter, longer than the last. Here was real
sport.

But wait! Of a sudden the pole was fairly yanked
from her hand. "A fish!" she exclaimed. "Oh! A
fish."

She reeled in rapidly. The fish came up from the
deep.

"Only a poor little four pound pike," she sighed as she shook him free.

The little pike had three brothers; at least she hooked that number and threw them back.

Then came a sudden shock. It was as if a powerful man had seized her lure and given it a terrific yank.

"That's the big boy again, or his brother." She was thinking of that other night with Jeanne. She set her shoulders for a tussle. "If it is—" She set her teeth tight. "Watch me land him!"

The "tussle" never rightly began. With a suddenness beyond power to describe, a voice in her very ear said:

"So! Now I have you!"

It was the man who meant to murder the aged moose. In his two gnarled hands he gripped a stout ashen oar. The oar was raised for a blow.

What had happened was this. Her mind fully occupied with the fishing adventure, the girl had allowed her boat to drift farther and farther into the bay. She had at last come within the stranger's view. Still angry because of his interrupted piece of vandalism, he had pushed off from the shore and, by using an oar for a paddle, had stolen upon her unobserved.

That there would be a battle the girl did not doubt. How would it end? Her pulse pounded madly as she reached for her own oar.

The two small boats were a full mile from the Narrows, through which one enters Duncan's Bay. At that moment a white fishing boat, fully forty feet long and gay with all manner of flags and bunting, was entering the Narrows.

There were a number of men and women on board, all gayly dressed and, until a few moments before, enjoying a grand fete of music and dancing. Now they were silent. Duncan's Bay affects all in this same manner. Dark, mysterious, deserted, it seems to speak of the past. A hush falls upon all alike as they pass between the narrow, sloping walls that stand beside the entrance to this place of strange enchantment.

Conspicuous because of his size and apparent strength, one man stood out from the other voyagers. Garbed in green breeches and a gayly decorated vest, he stood at the prow, massive brown arms folded, silently directing the course of the boat by a slight swaying, this way and that, of his powerful body.

Jane scarcely saw the strange ship. Her attention was held by the man in the rowboat. Jane was quick. Before the intruder could strike she had seized her oar and was prepared to parry the blow.

The oars came together with a solid thwack. Not a word was said as they drew back for a second sally.

This was to be a silent battle.

The man tried a straight on, sword-like thrust. It became evident at once that he meant to plunge her into the icy water.

Swinging her oar in a circle, she struck his weapon such a blow as all but knocked it from his hands.

Before he could regain his grip, she sent a flashing blow that barely missed his head, coming down with a thud upon his back.

Turning upon her a face livid with anger, he executed a crafty thrust to the right, leading her weapon stray. Before she could recover, her boat tipped. She fell upon one knee. At the same instant there came a crashing blow that all but downed her for a count of ten. The man smiled.

"I'm done!" her aching heart seemed to whisper.

"But what was this? There came the sound of heavy feet dropping upon the bottom of the boat. This was followed by a wolf-like growl. Then came the panting breath of terrific struggle.

Jane regained full consciousness in time to see her adversary caught in the grip of a powerful man, and to witness the feat of strength that lifted him clear of the boat and sent him sprawling into black waters a full ten feet away.

At that her deliverer turned and smiled, showing his fine white teeth.

"Bihari!" she exclaimed. "Bihari the gypsy!"

"Yes, Miss Jane." The man bowed. "Here we meet again. And this one—" He glanced at the man struggling in the water. "What of him?"

"It's not far to shore. Perhaps he can swim that far."

"Ah, yes, I am sure of that." Bihari's grin broadened. "Come then, we will forget him. You will come aboard our fine little schooner. My good Mama will look you over and see if you are hurt."

To her surprise Jane found the flag-bedecked boat close at hand. The villainous intruder had been outgeneraled by his own tactics. He had come upon Jane silently, unobserved. In this same manner Bihari, witnessing the struggle, had stolen upon him. Not, however, until he had won the battle had Bihari discovered he was defending a longtime friend.

"Jane!" his buxom wife cried as the girl climbed aboard. "It is indeed good to see you! And where is my Jeanne?"

"She—she's not far away. You shall see her within an hour if you choose."

"Choose?" Bihari laughed a great roaring laugh. "Have we not traveled half way round the world that we might see her? Have we not traded our vans for a boat that we might come to this place? Show us the way."

"You saw the wreck as you came in?"

"It's Bihari the Gypsy!" Jane Exclaimed

"Ah, yes."

"That is the place."

"The wreck?" Bihari stared.

"The wreck," she repeated.

Without another word this strange skipper mounted the deck to begin that unusual directing of his craft.

Four words came back to Jane, as with her boat in tow, she rode in luxurious ease out of the bay. "We will forget him." Bihari had said that. He had been speaking of the stranger. Could they safely forget him? Something seemed to tell her they could not.

CHAPTER ELEVEN

SONG OF THE PHANTOM

It is not difficult to imagine Jeanne's wild joy when, after an hour of disappointment because she had no boat for rowing to Duncan's Bay, she saw the gay gypsy boat slip from out the Narrows and head straight for the spot where she stood upon the sloping deck.

"Oh!" she cried to Greta. "They are coming! Jane has found them. She knows how I love gypsies who are good. She will bring them." She sprang into a dance so wild that Greta thought she would spin quite off the deck and go flying through the air to meet the gay white boat.

"It can't be Bihari!" she exclaimed at last, throwing herself down upon the deck. "It just cannot be!"

It was Bihari for all that. The schooner was still an arm's length from the side of the wreck when with one wild leap Jeanne was in Madame Bihari's strong arms.

"Jeanne! My Petite Jeanne!" the good woman cried. Tears stood in her eyes. "Jeanne, you are with us once more!"

There followed hours of great joy, of music and feasting; telling of stories, too.

"In France," Bihari told Jeanne, "all is not well. We came to America, and then to Chicago. You were not there. You had gone to Lake Superior for a vacation, your friends told us.

"We came to the shore of Lake Superior. You were not there. They said, 'She is on an island, Isle Royale.' We said, 'Take our vans. We must have a boat.' See! We have a boat. Is it not a jolly one? And we have you!

"And see!" he exclaimed, pointing at a brown mass of fur against the cabin. "See, we have brought your bear. Mama here has made him practice and he still knows your dances.

"Come!" he exclaimed, poking the sleeping bear with his foot. "Come! Dance for us!"

Unrolling himself, the bear stood up. At first, still groggy with sleep, he looked more like an empty sack trying to play it was a man. When Bihari seized his violin and began to play, it was as if the bear were run by a motor and the current was suddenly turned on. He began hopping about in a most grotesque manner. Soon he and Jeanne were doing a wild, weird dance.

Jane and Greta looked on silently. How strange all this was! What a different life these people led. Even Jeanne seemed to be another person.

"Bravo!" Bihari shouted when the dance was over. "We will visit the island. We will go to every place where there are people. They shall have music and dancing, such entertainment as they have never known before."

The days that followed were one round of joy for the little French girl. The old wreck became once more a pleasure ship. Flags and bunting were hung on every brace and spar. The deserted cabins overflowed with life and echoed sounds of joy from dawn to dark.

Great flat boxes of clay were brought from the mainland. On these campfires were kindled. Their red and yellow gleam might be seen wavering upon the water far and near. Strange dishes were prepared in kettles hung over these fires. They feasted, danced, sang, and told stories by the hour. Both Jeanne and Jane lived the life of Bihari and his band.

As for the dark-eyed Greta, it was all so wild and strange she could only sit shyly smiling in a corner, both charmed and bewildered by the ways of these people of the open road.

At times she stole away to the prow. One night, when songs were loudest, she took her violin from beneath her arm and played to the rushing waves. Then again she would sit staring away toward the land where no light shone, dreaming wonderful strange dreams.

"Gold," she would murmur, "a barrel of gold.

Jane said there might be a barrel of gold buried on the camping ground.

"But that," she would exclaim, "that is absurd!" In spite of all her denials, the conviction clung to her that somehow, somewhere a barrel of gold would play an important part in her life.

"I wonder how much that would be?" she murmured. "Enough for—for everything?" For a long time she had wished to study violin under a very great master, and had not been able.

"Money, money, money," she whispered now. "Some have much more than they need, and some none at all. How strange life is!"

Finding in this no source of joy, she gazed away toward the shores of Isle Royale, to dream that she was once more listening to the magic music of the phantom violin.

In this mood she took up her own violin and was soon lost to all else in an attempt to reproduce the notes of the haunting melody that had come to her that night.

To her unspeakable joy, she found she could catch here and there a few scattered notes. With time it came to her more and more.

So engrossed was she in this joyous adventure into the unknown, she did not know that the gypsy songs had ceased, that soft padded footsteps approached, that a little circle of eager listeners had gathered about her.

"Ah!" someone sighed as her last note died away on the breeze.

Then, in consternation, she became conscious of their presence.

"Magnificent!" Bihari exclaimed. "We have artists of the violin in France. Few play more wonderfully. What piece is that?"

"It—" Greta stared. "Why, that is the song of the phantom."

"Song of the phantom!"

"It must have been a phantom for Swen says no one lives up there on the ridge. But that is where the wonderful music came from. It was beautiful— more beautiful than I have ever heard before!" Greta told Bihari.

"That is no phantom!" Bihari declared stoutly. "Some great artist is hidden away in those hills. Why? I wonder. I should like very much to hunt him out and sit at his feet. But tomorrow—no, the day after—we become water gypsies again. We must play and dance. Coins must jingle, for we must have money to live.

"And you—" He turned eagerly to Jeanne. "You will go with us, round the island?"

"Yes! Yes! She will go. Jeanne will go!" The gypsy band, all old friends, swarmed about her. What else could she say but "Yes, I will go."

"And you," she cried, gathering Greta and Jane in her arms, "you will go also?"

"It would be a grand adventure," Jane replied, "but Greta is here, partly to rest and grow strong. I think we must stay and keep the ship until your return."

So in the end this was agreed upon. "And we," Greta whispered to Jane, "we shall go over to Duncan's Bay. We shall dig for a barrel of gold and hunt down the home of that phantom who plays so divinely."

"Yes," Jane agreed. "We will do just that." But in her own mind's eye was the face of a very ugly man. And that man had an oar raised menacingly above her head.

The next day was Sunday. There was no wild and hilarious music on this day, for Bihari and his band were deeply religious. All day they sat about the ship in groups talking quietly.

As darkness fell a bright fire was lighted. Bihari took down his violin and all joined in those sacred melodies that belong to all time, all lands, and all people.

The next day, with many a shout of farewell, the gypsy bark sailed away. And in the prow, standing beside Bihari, was the little French girl, her golden hair blowing in the wind.

"I'll be back in ten days," she shouted back as the

wreck began to grow small in the distance.

"I hope so," Jane whispered, "but I wonder if she'll want to come back, or if she'll like the gypsy life so well she will stay with them."

CHAPTER TWELVE

GOLD

Bihari and his gypsy band in their *Ship of Joy* had scarcely passed from sight around Blake's Point, when the sun went under a cloud and a damp, chill wind came driving in from the north.

"Boo! How cold!" Greta wrapped her sweater tight about her.

With the gay flags down, the hilarious music stilled, the wreck seemed a cold, dull and lifeless place. "There is something sinister and threatening about it," Jane thought.

To Greta she said, "Pack up the things you'll need for ten days, plenty of warm clothes. We're going camping on the island. We'll tramp all over Greenstone Ridge and sleep where night overtakes us."

"That," Greta cried, "will be grand! Shall I take my violin?"

"Surely. You might be able to take a few lessons from your mysterious phantom," Jane laughed as she began packing away eatables that were both light and nourishing.

"There are streams and small lakes," she murmured half to herself. "We shall have fish to fry, and some berries are ripe, blueberries, raspberries, and blackberries. Perhaps back in the woods we may even find some late strawberries."

In less than an hour the two girls had their packing finished and stowed away in the boat. After one last look around the wreck to see that everything was shipshape, they settled themselves in the boat. Jane took the oars, and in a moment they were started on their ten-day trip in search of adventure.

"Here," Jane said to Greta as her feet touched the shores of the camping ground on Duncan's Bay, "here we shall camp for the night. Tomorrow we will go on. I mean to do a little digging."

"For gold?" Greta stared at the girl, then laughed merrily.

"For a barrel of gold." Jane smiled. "Well, anyway, for something."

Dragging a small trench spade from the boat, she studied the lay of the land.

"Now where would one make camp?" she said thoughtfully as her keen eyes surveyed the narrow patch of ground. "Not too far back. The campfire might be blown into the forest and set the hillside blazing. Not too close to the shore either. The wind might come up and drive the waves over you while you slept.

"About here." She set her spade at the very center of the level stretch of ground that in all was not larger than one city lot.

"You know, Greta," she said thoughtfully as she began to dig, "it really doesn't matter whether we find a barrel of gold. Very often people are harmed by having too much money. It's good for us to work. There are ways of getting things we need—clothes, plain food, and all the education that's good for us, if we are wise and really work hard.

"We may find gold. No one could be sure we will not. We may find charcoal and scorched bones. If we study these carefully we can say, 'This fire was kindled two hundred years ago, before ever white men set foot on these shores.' We will be adding a sentence or two to Isle Royale's strange history. That's something.

"And we might—" she was digging now, cutting away the thin sod, then tossing out shovelfuls of sandy soil. "We might possibly find some copper instruments crudely made by the Indians.

"That—" She stood erect for a moment. "That would be a great deal. Any museum would pay well for those. Some may have been found on the island, but I doubt it. But it is known that the Indians came here from the mainland to take chunks of solid copper from the rocks.

"They had to heat the rock, build great fires upon it, then drag the fire away and crack the brittle hot rock.

"Copper!" She took a deep breath. "That's why

"We May Find Gold," Jane Told Her Companion

we have the island instead of Canada. History, Greta, is truly fascinating if you study it as we are doing now, right on the ground. We—what's that!" she broke off short. Some metal object had clinked on her spade.

"It's a coin!" she exclaimed a moment later. "A very old coin, I am sure!" She was all excitement. "Money! I told you, Greta! Gold!"

It was indeed a golden coin, very thin and quite small.

By careful scouring they managed to make out that the words stamped on its face were French. They could not read the date.

"Gold!" Greta seized the spade to begin digging vigorously. "Gold! There was a barrel of gold! The barrel rotted long ago. But the gold, it is still there. We will find it!"

In a very short time Greta found she was panting. She worked frantically, trying to keep pace with her racing imagination. Blisters were already showing themselves on her hands. That is the way Greta did everything. She put all her energy and imagination in the task before her. She might soon have exhausted herself had not Jane shoved her gently to one side and taken the spade from her.

Strangely enough, Jane had thrown out but three shovelfuls of sand when again her blade rang.

This time the earth yielded a greater treasure—

not gold, but copper. It was a small knife with a thin blade and a round handle of copper. The marks of the crude native smithy who fashioned it were on it.

"From the past!" Jane's eyes gleamed. "The very distant past! How Doctor Cole of the museum at home will exclaim over that!"

So engrossed were the two girls in their study of this new treasure, they failed to note three facts. Darkness had fallen. The line of the forest was black against the late twilight sky. A stealthy figure was creeping slowly toward them, keeping well-hidden in the dark shadows of the great trees. And a small, powerful motorboat had entered the Narrows of the bay and was headed for the shore where the girls were making their camp for the night.

In the meantime Jeanne had made an important discovery. The *Ship of Joy* had gone cruising round Blake's Point to turn in at a narrow circular bay known as Snug Harbor.

Jeanne thought this one of the most beautiful spots she had ever known. There was a white lodge building, more than half hidden by fir and balsam, and little cottages were tucked away at the edge of the forest, and about it all there was an air of quiet and peace. They were at the door of Rock Harbor Lodge.

"We will disturb their quiet," Jeanne thought to

herself, "but not their peace, I am sure."

While Bihari was talking with the owner of the lodge regarding a night of music and dancing, she stole away over a path shadowed by mountain ash and fir. At the end of the path she came to a long, low, private cottage, boarded up and closed. Before this house a long narrow dock ran out into the bay. Tied to this dock was a schooner.

"The black schooner!" Jeanne shuddered.

Yet drawn toward it by curiosity, she walked slowly down the dock to find herself at last peering inside the long, low cabin.

At once she sprang back as if she had seen someone. But no one was there. The schooner was for the moment deserted. What she had seen, hanging against the wall, was a diver's helmet.

"The black schooner! The one that came to the wreck the other night," she murmured once more as she hurried away, losing herself from sight in the shadow of the forest.

Jeanne wandered about for a while then made her way back toward the dock where the gypsy ship was tied.

When Jeanne once more reached the lodge dock, a crowd of people from the cottages had gathered about Bihari and his band. She grasped the sleeve of a tall young man and pointed to the closed cottage. "Do you know what schooner that is?" she managed to say to him in a low voice.

"Schooner?" He smiled down at her.

"Yes, the one by that other dock. Over—why!" she exclaimed, "it is gone! It was a black schooner. But now it is not there."

The tall young man looked at her in a manner that seemed to say, "You've been seeing things."

This embarrassed her, so she lost herself in the crowd.

But not for long. One moment, and a pleasing voice was saying in her ear, "And are you the golden-haired gypsy who will dance with the bear tonight?"

CHAPTER THIRTEEN

THE HEAD HUNTER

Back on the camping ground, the first intimation Jane and Greta had that there was anyone about was when, with a startling suddenness, a bright searchlight flashed into their eyes. The light came from the water. At the same time there came the sound of movement in the dry leaves of the forest at their backs. Instinctively Jane whirled about. Her bright eyes searched the forest. No one was there.

When the searchlight from the water had been switched off, Jane saw the dark gray power boat approaching the camping ground.

"Greta," she groaned, "we should have gone up the ridge at once! There's no peace or privacy anywhere!"

As the boat came nearer they read in large letters across the prow one word, "CONSERVATION."

This brought momentary relief to the startled girls. Conservation men are government men and these, Jane believed, could be trusted.

Pulling in close to shore, the boat dropped anchor. A sturdy, sun-tanned man leaped into the small boat they had in tow, and rowed rapidly toward land.

"Who's the man who went into the bush just

now?" he demanded of the girls the instant his feet touched land.

"M—man?" Jane stammered. "There is no man."

"So I see," the newcomer grumbled. "There was one, though. Don't try to deceive me! I saw him! He's short, stoutly built, rather dark, with a week's beard. Now then! Does that convince you?"

"Yes." Jane found her knees trembling. "Perhaps," she thought, "these Conservation men have saved us from trouble without knowing it."

"Yes," she repeated, "I believe you are telling the truth. You did see a man. But—but he doesn't belong to us. Truly he does not! Wait! I'll tell you about him for I think it must be the same one I saw a few days ago."

"Tell me about yourself first. What are you doing here?" The man did not smile.

"Why—we—we—we—" Jane was greatly disturbed. "We came over here from the wreck. We—"

"Oh!" her inquisitor broke in as a smile overspread his face. "You're the girls living out there on the wreck. That—er—I owe you an apology. We've heard of you. You're O. K. You see, we're the Conservation men on the island, Dick and I. We've got to see that no game is killed, no trees cut, no fires started, all that.

"But tell me now—" His voice took on an eager note. "Tell me about that man."

Jane told him all she knew. He was, she felt quite certain, the man who had intended murdering Old Uncle Ned, the veteran moose, and the man who had fought with her that battle of oars. She trembled now as she thought what might have happened to them that night had not these Conservation men happened along.

"Excuse me," the Conservation man said when the story was done. "My name is Mell. As man to man, I'd like to shake your hand. The way you saved the old moose was keen. You're the right sort. I—I'll get you a job on our force." He shook her hand warmly.

"But this fellow—" his brow wrinkled. "We'll have to look after him. He's a head hunter, beyond a doubt. Fellow can get good money for a fine pair of moose antlers. These rascals come over here and kill our best friends of the wildwood, just for a few dollars. Watch us go after him!"

Leaping into his boat, he was away.

"He's—he's all right." Jane was enthusiastic. "The question is, shall we camp here or try a return trip to the ship?" For a moment all thoughts of the treasure hunt were forgotten as the girls studied their present problem.

They soon had a glowing bed of coals in the shallow pit where they had built their fire. Over the coals they put bacon to broil. The smell of the siz-

"Tell Me About That Man," He said Eagerly

zling bacon, mingled with the tangy odor of the pines, reminded them how hungry they were.

"The moon will be out by ten o'clock," Jane said after a moment's thought. "It will be safer on the water then. We'll try to get back to the wreck then."

Their evening lunch over, the girls curled up side by side with the wall of their small tent at their back and the glowing fire before them. All about them was blackness. Not a gleam came from the surface of dark waters. Not a break appeared in the wall of deep green that was the forest at their back. For all this, they were not afraid. Swen's rifle lay across Jane's knees. Their ears were keen. No intruder could slip upon them unannounced.

"Gold!" Greta whispered, already half asleep. "We found a tiny bit. I wonder if there can be much more."

"Who knows?" Jane murmured dreamily.

Presently her head fell forward and she was asleep.

Greta did not wake her. "I will hear in time if there is any danger," she told herself. She liked the feel of all this, the warmth of the fire on her face, the little breezes playing in her hair, her sleeping comrade, the night, the mysterious forest—all this seemed part of a new world to her. She smiled as she thought of her own soft bed at home with its bright covers and downy pillow. "Who would wish to live like that always?" she asked herself. "Who—"

Her thoughts snapped off like a radio singer who had been cut off. Wind was beginning to come down the bay and, wafted along by it was a sound, faint, indistinct but unmistakable.

"The phantom violin!" she whispered.

This time the sound came from so great a distance that it was but a teasing phantom of sound.

Greta sat up quietly. She wanted to slip away into the forest and follow the sound. But she dared not. She remained perfectly quiet, almost holding her breath as she listened intently to the clear, sweet music.

As Greta listened, Jane awoke and blinked her eyes sleepily.

"What's the matter?" she asked. "Did you hear something? Is the head hunter back?"

"Shhh! Listen!" commanded Greta.

Jane listened intently. Faintly from the forest came the sweet, clear notes of a violin. For several minutes the girls listened. Then the notes died away and there was no sound but the lapping of the water on the sand and the sighing of the wind in the tree-tops.

"Did you hear him?" Greta asked breathlessly.

"Yes," murmured Jane. "So that is the phantom violin. That is the sound we are going to search for."

For a few minutes the girls sat quite still listening, but the song of the phantom violin was finished for that evening. Their eyes grew heavy and soon both girls were asleep.

That same evening Petite Jeanne was with her wild, free friends of other days. In the pale light of Chinese lanterns she danced with the bear the old fantastic dances of those other days. When it was over and she passed the tambourine for Bihari, a great weight of silver coins thumped into it. For a while she was deliriously happy. When it was all over and she had rowed alone in a small boat out to the center of the narrow bay, her feelings changed. For one short moment she wished herself back on the wreck with Jane and Greta.

"But I must not!" She pulled herself up short. "Bihari and his people have done much for me. I must not fail them now.

"Ah! But this is beautiful!" she breathed a moment later. "And I shall see it all—all this marvelous island!"

The scene before her was like some picture taken from a fairy book. Through the dark circle of forest only a pale light gleamed here and there like a star, and at the center of all this the lights of a long, low room cast mellow reflections upon the water.

Figures moved about like gay phantoms in this light. To her ears came the low melody of guitar and violin.

"It is so beautiful!" She felt her throat tighten with the joy of it all. "And yet—"

She was thinking of the black schooner that had slipped away into the great unknown lying away beyond the shrouds of night.

"The diver was on that schooner," she assured herself. "What if they return to our home, our poor wrecked ship! They may set fire to it! They may blow it up with dynamite!" She shuddered. "They came there to look for something. I wonder what it could be? What is on that ship that anyone would want?"

The more Jeanne thought of the black schooner and the diver, the more determined she became that when the three girls returned to the *Pilgrim* they must examine every part of the wreck thoroughly. Perhaps Swen would help them. At any rate, they *must* find out what these men wanted on the ship.

But someone was calling her name. She must return to the shore. Her brief hour of reverie was at an end.

On the camping grounds at Duncan's Bay Jane slept for two hours. Greta, too, woke when she heard Jane stirring. When she woke the moon was out. The wind too had risen.

"We can't get back to the wreck tonight; the waves will be too high," was her instant decision.

"We must stay here for the night."

"And tomorrow," Greta whispered eagerly, "tomorrow at dawn we will go up the ridge."

"Why so soon?"

"I am so anxious to find the owner of the phantom violin," Greta replied. "We must start as soon as we can."

"We shall see," said Jane, and began preparation for the night.

Their tent was small, only six feet square. It had a floor of canvas. Once inside with the flap buttoned tight, they were as securely housed as the caterpillar in his chrysalis.

Greta was not slow in creeping down among the blankets. She went to sleep at once.

As for Jane, she drew on her heavy sweater, thrust her feet under the blankets, propped the rifle against the tent wall and, folding her arms across her knees, sat at half watch the night through.

The sun had not cleared the treetops when the Conservation boat appeared. It had a small black power boat in tow.

"We waited for him all night, that head hunter," Mell explained. "He didn't show up. He must have hoofed it back into the hills, I guess. The boat was stolen. We're taking it back.

"No good, his hiding in the forest," he concluded. "We'll get him, you'll see. We'll tell every ship captain to watch for him. You needn't be afraid. We'll find him before the day is over."

With that the men pulled away and with a few put, puts from their motorboat they were out of sight around the curve of the shore line.

"I hope," said Jane when they were gone, "that they get him very soon."

A half hour later, with packs on their backs, the two girls headed up the rocky slope.

"The treasure hunt can wait," was Jane's comment. "We can go after that when Jeanne is back. Now we're going to explore Greenstone Ridge, and search for the phantom violin."

CHAPTER FOURTEEN

THE SECRET OF GREENSTONE RIDGE

Late the next afternoon the *Ship of Joy* with **Bihari** and his band, including Jeanne and the bear, went gliding down the long narrow stretch of water known as Rock Harbor. As Jeanne, seated in a sunny spot on the deck, watched the small island to the left go gliding by, she felt, as one feels the current of galvanic electricity go coursing through his system, the thrill and mild terror that comes when one senses impending adventure, terror, or disaster. She could not tell what was to happen.

"Something will happen," a voice seemed to whisper. "You are coming nearer and nearer."

She did not doubt the voice. It had come to her before. Such is the gift of wandering people; they feel and know in advance.

No, she did not doubt. And yet, the low sun shone so mildly, waves lapped the boat's sides so dreamily, islands of green and brown glided by so like drifting shadows, she forgot all else and, stretching out upon the deck, she surrendered herself to the spell of it all.

The calm, dreamy mood of Lake Superior did not last long. A chill wind came sweeping over the tops

114

of the islands. Dark clouds scurried overhead.

"This is bad!" Bihari grumbled. "Our next stop is Chippewa Harbor. We must go out into the lake to get there. Lake Superior is bad when he is angry. He puts out hands and seizes small boats. He drags them down and they are never seen again.

"At Chippewa Harbor there are little cabins and just now a large party camping in tents. We will sing and dance for them.

"But tomorrow—" he laughed a large, good-natured laugh. "Tomorrow. We have with us always tomorrow. That will do.

"In this harbor we are safe. Tonight we will sing for ourselves."

He was right. When at last they reached the narrow passage through which they were to glide into broad, open waters, they saw an endless field of black and white, a stormy sea.

Pulling in behind a small island where the wind could not reach them and the water was at rest, they dropped anchor and at once the gypsy band was engaged in a merry and quite innocent revel of wild music.

Jeanne did not join them. She did not know exactly why, but she did not feel like dancing and singing. She thought of Jane and Greta. She wondered if they were at the wreck or on land, and wondered, too, how the wreck would stand the storm. She thought of friends in Chicago and her castle in France where her foster parents saw to it that she lived up to her position as a great young lady.

"If things had been different, if there had been no war, where would I be now?

"But that's enough of that idle thinking," she said to herself. She shook her head to drive away the unwelcome imaginings. "I like it here. Everything is beautiful; Bihari is kind and good; and I have many friends."

Suddenly she jumped to her feet and with a wild fling she swung into a gypsy dance. For a few minutes she spun gayly about the deck, then as suddenly as she had started she stopped.

"The abandoned lighthouse!" she cried. "That is where our good friend the fisher boy, Swen, lives. He told me he had his home with his father and mother in that tower. What an odd home it must be! No corners in the rooms at all. Oh, I must see it and our friend, Swen!"

The next instant she sprang into a boat bumping at the side of the schooner, untied the rope, seized the oars and rowed away alone. Even as she did this there came over her again that sense of impending danger.

Greenstone Ridge, like the backbone of a very lean horse, runs the entire length of Isle Royale. The

Jeanne Swung into a Gypsy Dance

crest of that ridge may be reached only by climbing a very steep slope. This climb is broken by narrow plateaus. When Jane and Greta had reached the first plateau, they turned their backs upon that end of the island that was known to them, and headed straight on into the great unknown.

They came at once upon a well-trodden moose trail. Hundreds of moose wander from end to end of this strange island. This trail made travel easy. Moss soft as carpet, bits of soft wood beaten into pulp, with here and there a stretch of black earth or gray rock, offered pleasant footing for their patiently plodding feet.

"We'll stop at noon," Jane said, "and have a cold lunch and a good rest. We'll travel some more after that. When we're tired we'll find a big flat rock, build a fire, make hot chocolate, fry bacon, and have a real feast. Then the tent and blankets. We'll be living where no one has lived. We'll be explorers. Won't it be grand?"

Greta had thought it might be. She did not feel quite sure. Pictures of her own safe bed, of a table spread with snowy linen and shining silver, floated before her eyes. "If mother could see me now!" she whispered and smiled to herself.

"But, oh, it is good to breathe—just breathe!" Throwing back her shoulders, she drank in a breath of air that was like water, clear and cold from a deep well.

On this long tramp Jane led the way. Never a person who would waste breath with idle talk on such an occasion, she plodded along in silence. For all that, her active brain was busy. She was thinking through a very special and private interview she had had with Swen, the fisher boy, only three days before.

"So you are going way back up yonder?" He had waved a sun-browned arm toward the distant ridge.

"Yes." Jane had caught her breath. "Yes, we are going up there. Won't it be gr-a-a-nd! They say no one goes up there—that perhaps no one has ever been up there. It must be lonely, silent, beautiful!"

"It's all of that." The fisherman's blue eyes were frank and kind. "But I thought I'd ought to tell you, just in case you don't know, there's someone waiting for you up there."

"No." The girl spoke quickly. "No, there is no one at all. We are going by ourselves, just Greta and I. We sent no one ahead."

"I believe you," Swen replied. "All the same, there's someone up there. I'll tell you how I know."

As if to collect his thoughts, he had paused, looking away at Greenstone Ridge. Jane recalled that now.

It was worth looking at, that ridge. In truth, every little corner of this large island was worth looking at.

Just then the setting sun had transformed the far-away green of spruce and balsam into a crown of green and gold.

"I'll tell you why I know there's someone up there," Swen went on presently. "I've got a little store down by the end of the harbor. Four times that store has been entered. Things have been taken. Not stolen; just taken and the money left to pay for them. The first three times it was food they took. The last time it was a grinding stone for polishing greenstone. Cost me five dollars. The five was there. Can you beat that?"

"But your store is on the other side of the island," Jane had protested. "That's another place entirely. We're not going there."

"It's all the same ridge," Swen explained, patient-ly. "When you come to the tip-top of the ridge and if you go far enough toward the center of the island —not so far, either—you can look down on Duncan's Bay on your side and upon our harbor on the other.

"And up there somewhere," he added with con-viction, "there's someone. I know it! He took things from our store."

Jane had thought of Greta's phantom. Could it be that there truly was someone living on this ridge? And would they discover that person?

"He pays for things he takes. He is honest," she argued to herself. "He loves music. No true musician could be unkind or brutal."

"But, after all," she had insisted, turning her face to Swen, "after all, there is no one. A boat came along at night. The people in the boat took the things from your store."

"Came in a boat, that's what I thought at first." The light of mystery shone in the fisherman's eye. "But the last time, that time he took the grinding wheel and left the five dollars in gold, there was a storm on old Superior, a terrible nor'easter. No one could have lived in that sea. And there wasn't so much as a rowboat in the harbor.

"And that person doesn't live on the shore, either," he went on after a moment. "I know every boat of the shore, I do. Naturally, then, they're up there on Greenstone Ridge somewhere, someone is, that's certain."

"How—how long ago?" The words had stuck in Jane's throat.

"First time was all of a year ago. Last time, early this spring."

"Then—then perhaps he's gone. This is August, you know."

"Maybe he's gone, miss. Somehow I don't think so."

"Why would anyone want to stay a whole year in such a place? Just think what it would mean!" Jane's eyes opened wide. "They would have no companions. There would be no food except that which they brought in from the village. All during the winter they would be snowed in. And all year round there would be no one to talk to. They would be all alone!"

"You're assuming there's only one. I don't know. There might be more. Articles have been found missing from cottages closed for the winter, food and clothing. Always paid for, though. One fisherman, who was very poor, found the price of three pairs of boots left for one pair; well-worn ones they were, too.

"But why do they stay up there?" he went on. "It's your question. Perhaps you will find the answer."

"Wh—why haven't you been up there to see?" Jane asked.

"Me? See here, miss, I'm a fisherman. I belong to the water. No land lubberin' for me! And besides, I've a father and mother to look after. I got my money for the things he took, didn't I? Then what call do I have looking into places like that?"

Once again the girl had looked away to the place where the ridge must be. It was gone, swallowed up in the night. Not a light had shone up there. Not a campfire gleamed.

"There is no one up there," she had whispered to herself as she stood alone on the deck of the wrecked ship, straining her eyes for even a very small gleam against the sky. "There can't be. They'd have a lamp of some sort, even if it were only a pine-knot torch.

"Swen must have been mistaken. Whoever took his things must have come from a boat or from the shore. There just couldn't be anyone living up there on the ridge."

Then of a sudden she had thought of the curious green light Greta had seen at a distance on that very ridge.

"What could have caused that light?" she had asked herself.

She asked it all over again as she trudged away over the moose trail.

"Of course," she thought, "there's the head hunter. But he's out. Such men don't climb ridges unless they're obliged to—too lazy for that! And they don't make divine music nor light green lamps at night.

"I suppose," she whispered to herself after a time, "I should have told Greta what Swen said, but—"

Well, she just hadn't wanted to, that was all. Perhaps she had been selfish, she had wanted this trip so much. She had wanted company too. And too much talk about the secrets of Greenstone Ridge might have frightened Greta out altogether.

"Do you know why they call this Greenstone Ridge?" she said aloud to Greta.

"No. Why?"

"Because there is a kind of quartz embedded in some of the rocks. They call these greenstones. They are about the seventh most valuable stone in the world."

"Shall we find some?" Greta's tone was eager.

"We'll hope so." Jane shifted her pack. "They make grand stones for rings, or pins or things like that. You chip them from the rocks with a chisel or hatchet."

"Greenstones," Greta whispered to herself. "Green stone and a green light on this very ridge. Of course, there's no connection; but then, it's sort of strange."

CHAPTER FIFTEEN

A LEAP IN THE DARK

Jeanne's row from the *Ship of Joy* to the small dock before the ancient lighthouse was a short one. Her boat tied up, she hurried along the dock, then over the winding path leading up the gentle slope.

Darkness was falling. Even now, from the schooner's cabin she caught a yellow gleam of light. She cast a hurried glance toward the tall stone tower.

"They live up there somewhere," she murmured. "But there's no light."

She quickened her step. "It will soon be dark."

Hesitating before a door, she took a grip on herself, then seized the doorknob and gave it a quick turn. The door flew open. Silence, the faint smell of smoked fish, and half darkness greeted her. She was at the foot of a winding stairway. She sprang forward and up. At the top of that stairway was a second door. It stood ajar. She rapped on it. No answer. A louder rap. Still no answer.

"I'll just make sure." She pushed the door open. "Yes," she told herself, "someone lives here, some old people who love comfort, chairs and soft, home-made cushions and all that. Dear old people they must be. And there, there's a rag doll! There must be children, too. Swen never spoke of them. Perhaps—"

She was beginning to think she had come to the wrong lighthouse, when a sound from the stairs caused her to start violently.

"Who—who's there?" Her voice shook ever so slightly.

There came no answer. Instinctively the girl sprang toward the center of this tower room. Just why she was frightened she could not say.

Perhaps this movement saved her. As she whirled about she saw to her horror that there, standing in the doorway, was the head hunter. She had not seen him before, but from Jane's description she knew she could not be mistaken. There was the same short, stout body, the dark, evil face, the bloodshot eyes. That he recognized her as Jane's friend she could not doubt. There was a look of savage glee in his eyes.

For a space of seconds the little French girl stood paralyzed with fear. Then as her eyes circled the room they caught sight of a second door. She sprang toward this.

The door swung open and banged shut. Like a flash she was away up a second flight of stairs.

"This leads to the top of the tower," she told herself. "And when I'm out there?"

A bat, frightened from the beams, flashed by her,

The Head Hunter Was Standing in the Doorway

another, and still another. She hated and feared
bats. But a greater terror lay behind. There came
the sound of heavy steps.

Darkness lay before her. "A trap door." Her
frightened mind recorded these words. "What if it
is locked?"

It was not locked. She was through it. It slammed
behind her. There was no lock on that side. What
was to be done?

Two heavy stones on the ledge beside her seemed
loose. They *were* loose. Pushing more than lifting,
she banged one down upon the door, then the other.
She caught the sound of muttered curses as the second stone banged down.

Safe for the moment, she considered her next
move. That the man would, in time, be able to
wreck that door she did not doubt.

"There's sure to be an axe down there," she told
herself.

Wildly her eyes searched the circular platform.
In an obscure spot she saw a coil of rope.

"It's stout," she told herself, "but too short. It
would never reach the ground." Dizzily she surveyed
the scene below. Beneath her for the most part were
rocks. Between these were narrow patches of grass.
"That's a nice place to land!" she grumbled.

To the right and some twenty feet from the tower
was a huge fir tree. In her distress she fancied that

its branches reached out to her, offering aid.

"If only I could!" she murmured.

Seizing the rope, she tied one end to a beam, then leaning far out, watched the other end drop as it unfolded coil by coil. This came to an end at last. "It is still thirty feet to the ground," she thought with fresh panic. "I would be killed sure."

Standing quite still, she listened. There came no sound. "He's gone down. He may not come back." She uttered a low prayer that he would not.

She was thinking now, wondering how this man had come here, all the way across the ridge from Duncan's Bay. "Probably someone was after him. There should be," she told herself. "He probably came here to escape. He—"

Breaking in upon her thoughts came a terrific crash. A blow had been aimed at the trap door.

"He's found an axe. The door won't last." She was half way over the ledge. Ten seconds later, bracing her feet against the wall, she was going down the rope hand over hand.

The end? She reached that soon enough. She was still thirty feet above the earth, and clung there motionless.

Then of a sudden, taking a strong grip on the rope, she began working her way back, round the tower. When she had gone as far as she dared, she gave a quick, strong push and set herself swinging wide.

With a sort of pumping motion, aided by an occasional kick at the wall, she was able to get herself into a wide swing. Then of a sudden, with a quick intake of breath, she let go.

She fell, as she had hoped to do, squarely into the arms of the friendly fir tree. She caught at its branches, swayed forward, held her grip, shifted her feet, then sank to a deep, dark corner where, for the moment, she might rest and gain control of her wildly beating heart.

Ten seconds later there came a low swish. That was the falling rope. The head hunter had cut it. At the thought of what might have happened, the girl all but lost her balance.

A moment later, after a hasty scramble, she reached earth and went swiftly away.

With hands scratched, dress torn and heart beating wildly, she reached the dock, raced along on tiptoe, dragged the tie rope free, dropped into her boat, then rowed rapidly and silently away toward the gypsy boat.

Arrived at the side of the *Ship of Joy,* she drew her boat into its protective shadows to sit there watching, listening, waiting motionless.

From the shore there came a sound. It was a strange sound. She could not interpret it. In time it died away.

"Perhap I should tell Bihari all about it," she thought soberly. Still she did not move. She respected and loved the gallant gypsy chief; but most of all she feared his terrible anger.

"This," she thought with a shudder, "is no time for battle and bloodshed." Her eyes were fixed upon the dark masses of Greenstone Ridge. The moon in all its shining golden glory had just risen over that ridge.

On that ridge at this moment, had she but known it, sat two silent watchers, Jane and Greta. Had they been possessed of a powerful searchlight and an equally powerful telescope, they might have looked down from their lofty throne upon the little French girl seated there in the boat.

As Jeanne sat there a curious sound struck her ear. "It sounds like someone swimming," she told herself. "Surely that terrible man would not think of attempting to come here! He knows Bihari's power."

She sat motionless, listening, ready to spring up and flee, while the sound grew louder. Then of a sudden she gave vent to a low laugh.

"It must have been the bear!" she exclaimed in a whisper.

"The bear." Her tone was suddenly sober. "He has been on shore. How did he get away? What has he seen? What has he done?"

"Well!" She rose as, without seeing her, the bear tumbled clumsily over the schooner's rail. "Whatever he knows, he never will tell. That's where a bear makes a fine friend."

CHAPTER SIXTEEN

GRETA'S SECRET

That night the dark-eyed Greta found herself in the midst of a nature lover's paradise. Yet she was not at that moment thinking of any paradise. She was listening intently, listening to the sounds of the night, waiting, too, for some other sound that she hoped might come.

"Will it play tonight," she whispered to herself, "the phantom violin?"

That her ear might catch the faintest sound, she was sitting up in bed. And such a sweet-scented bed as it was! Blankets were spread over a thick mattress of dry moss and balsam tips.

"Why can't I forget the phantom violin and fall asleep?" she asked herself.

Once again she leaned forward to listen. "How sweet!" she murmured as she caught the night call of some small bird, a single long-drawn note. "Just a call in the night."

And then, muscles tense, ears strained, she sat erect.

"There it is again!"

It was no bird this time, no single note, but many notes. Yet it was all so indistinct.

133

"The phantom violin!" Her lips trembled. "Like the singing of angels!" she told herself.

"There, now it has faded away." Regret was registered in her tone.

Once again she crept under the blankets to the warm spot at Jane's side.

They had come far that day, with packs on their backs over rough moose trails. Jane, more used to tramping than Greta, had not seemed to mind the climb. She had rolled herself in her blankets and in two minutes was sleeping soundly.

Although Greta, too, was very tired, the strangeness of the place seemed to keep her awake. Her ears caught every rustle and sigh of the forest.

The spot they had chosen for their night camp was down from the very crest of Greenstone Ridge but a dozen paces.

Greta was very weary. They had traveled farther that day than had been their intention. There were no fit camping places along the moose trail. At last, just as shadows were falling, they had decided to climb to the crest, a hard task for the day's end. They had made it, for all that. And on the far side of that ridge they had discovered a perfect spot for a camp. A flat rock, some twenty feet across, offered support for an improvised hearth of stones. A mossy bed above this invited them to sleep.

"There's plenty of wind. We'll have no rain to-

"The Phantom Violin!" Greta Murmured

night," had been Jane's prophecy. "We'll pitch our tent here for tonight."

And so, here they were, and here was Greta, sitting up, wide awake, dreaming in the night.

Jane had known Greta for only a short time. She did not know how this quiet girl would react to danger or the thought of danger.

The story Swen had told Jane could not have frightened Greta from taking a part in this great adventure. The truth was, she knew it all, and more. She treasured a secret all her own. She was thinking of it now.

"He called them white flares," she murmured low. "Said if we were in grave danger or needed help in any way, to light one of them. He would see the white light against the sky and come. Vincent Stearns said that."

She had met Vincent Stearns, a sturdy, sun-tanned young man, a famous newspaper camera man, at Tobin's Harbor only two days before. Swen had taken her to the Harbor in his fishing boat. On the way he had told her of the mysterious someone who, he was sure, lived on Greenstone Ridge. She had repeated the story to Vincent Stearns.

"Yes," the photographer had said, "I've heard the story myself. So you are going up there on a camping trip—just two girls?" He had arched his brows.

"Oh, but you should see Jane!" Greta had

exclaimed. "She's capable. She always knows just what to do. Nothing will hurt us while she's along."

"All the same," he had insisted, "you may find yourself in need of help. Take these. They are white flares. If you need help, set one on a flat rock atop the ridge and set it off. I use 'em for taking pictures of moose at night. It can be seen for miles, that white light.

"I'm going to be hunting moose with a camera on the lakes near the far end of Rock Harbor. Wherever you are, if I see that flare I'll come."

Greta had accepted the white flares. They were in her kit bag now. "Not that we'll need them. But then, you never can tell," she thought.

After listening a long time for the return of the bewitching phantom music, she cuddled down and fell asleep.

It was at about this same hour that Jeanne, looking from her porthole in the *Ship of Joy*, watching the brown old lighthouse tower that stood all dark in the moonlight, saw at one of the windows a wavering light. This was followed by a steady yellow gleam.

"Who is it?" she asked herself. "Is that truly Swen's home? And has he returned? Or is that the head hunter making himself comfortable for the night?"

One more problem returned to her before she fell asleep. The bear had been to the mainland. Doubtless he had missed her and had followed by swimming. He had not, however, returned for some time. What had he done there on land?

"Probably nothing," she told herself. She could not be sure, however.

Greta had not slept long before she found herself once more wide awake, staring up at the fleeing clouds. "Something must have awakened me," she murmured. "What can it have been?"

Then, as minds have a way of doing, her mind took up an old, old problem and thought it all through again. This problem had to do with her future. A very rich woman had heard her playing the violin in a small concert. She had, as she had expressed it, been "charmed, charmed indeed," by Greta's playing. She had offered to become Greta's good angel.

"You shall study at my expense, under the very great masters," she had said. "No expense shall be spared. And in time—" her bulging eyes had glowed. "In time you shall have the whole world at your feet!"

Greta had not said, "I will do it." Instead, she had replied, "I must talk it over with my mother. I will see."

She was still "seeing." This was one of the problems yet to be solved. She did long to study under great masters. And yet, she loved her own family. She wished that they might do for her all that was grand and glorious. "To invite a rich stranger into one's life," some wise person had said to her, "is often to shut one's humble friends out."

"The world at my feet," she repeated, then laughed softly to herself. Beneath them, rolling away like billows of the sea, was the glorious green of that primeval forest; and beyond that, black and mysterious in the night, lay the calm waters of Lake Superior.

"The world at my feet! I have that tonight!" she murmured. "Down there, the forest, the lake, there is the world at my feet."

She sat straight up to listen. The wind had changed. It was rising. The right side of their tent was sagging. Borne in on this wind, the sound that had puzzled her before came sweeping in like the notes of some long-forgotten song.

"It's the 'Intermezzo' from 'Cavalleria Rusticana'!" Her astonishment knew no bounds. Surely there *was* someone on Greenstone Ridge! Someone who played the violin divinely.

"And yet," she thought more soberly, "in this still air sound carries far. It may be on some boat out there on the black waters."

Peering into the night she strained her eyes in a vain attempt to discover a light on the lake. There was no light.

She had just snuggled down in her warm corner once more when every muscle of her supple form stiffened in terror. She sprang to her feet. From some distant spot, yet startling in its distinctness, had come one wild, piercing scream.

"Wha—what could that have been?" she shuddered. She stood there wondering; then as the cold air crept around her, she lay down with a shiver and pulled the blankets about her. "Boo! How cold it is!"

Her mind was in a turmoil. Who had screamed? That it was a person, not some wild creature, she could not doubt. But who?

Should she waken Jane? Her hand was on the girl's shoulder. "But why?" she asked herself. "We are but two girls. What can we do in the night on a ridge we do not know? We might fall into a crevice and be of no help to anyone."

Once again she crawled down beneath the blankets. Once more she caught the notes of that mysterious music. It had not stopped. Plainly that person was not associated in any way with the scream. Then there must be two people on Greenstone Ridge.

The wind began whispering in the pines. The

sound blended with that strange music. Together they became the accompaniment to a dream. Greta slept. And still at her feet lay the glorious little world that is Isle Royale.

CHAPTER SEVENTEEN

THE CAVERN OF FIRE

Not until her courage had been strengthened by a steaming cup of coffee brewed over a fire before the tent, was Greta ready to tell her companion of the mysterious sounds in the night.

"It was only a crazy old loon," was Jane's prompt solution.

"A loon may be a bright bird," Greta said laughingly; with the light of day terror had vanished, "but I've never known a loon that can play the 'Intermezzo' from 'Cavalleria Rusticana.'"

"You know what I mean." Jane threatened her mockingly with her sheath knife. "It was a loon that screamed. They sound very human at times."

"Not as human as that cry in the night," the slender girl affirmed with conviction. "I'll never rest until I've solved the mystery of that cry."

Jane scrambled to her feet. "In that case, we'd better get at its solving at once."

"I guess that's right," Greta answered. "Let's get things picked up and be on our way."

Packing away their blankets, cleaning up their breakfast dishes and putting their camp in order took but a short time. Jane picked up a stout walking stick, and brandished it merrily in the air.

"Come on," she said. "We're off in search of a scream." And she led the way into the unknown forest.

"You said there are greenstones to be found right up here in the rocks." Greta studied a massive boulder of greenish hue.

"Yes." Jane produced a chisel and a small hammer. "Swen gave me these. They chisel the stones right out of the rocks. I saw one a lady down at Tobin's Harbor had set in a ring. It was a beauty. Worth quite a lot, I guess. Well, I hope to find a number as good as that. What grand Christmas presents they'd make!"

"Jane!" Greta came to a sudden halt. "Swen said someone took an emery wheel for grinding greenstones from his store. Do you suppose someone is up here hunting greenstones? And do you think he could have fallen off into a chasm or something last night? Was it his scream I heard?"

"So Swen told you all about that?" Jane exclaimed. "And yet you wanted to come!"

"I—wanted to come?" Greta stared at her. "Surely! Why not? More than ever!"

"Brave little girl!" Jane put a hand on her shoulder. "But that idea of yours about the scream seems a bit fantastic. You never can tell, though. But if he did fall in a crevice, we'd never find him, not up here.

"Look at that ledge!" She pointed away to the right. "It's a hundred feet high, half a mile long.

"And look down there." Her gaze swept the tangled forests that lay below the narrow plateau on which they stood. "Just look! Trees have been fighting for their lives there a thousand years. Twisted, tangled, fallen, grown over with bushes and vines. How is one to conduct a search in such a place? We might as well forget it."

"I guess you're right." Greta sighed. Nevertheless, she did not forget.

"Do you know," she said a moment later, "I believe I'd rather sit by our campfire and think than to go prowling round this ridge today."

"You're not afraid? Afraid of meeting some—someone?"

"Of course not! Just footsore and weary after yesterday."

"Yes, I suppose you are. I'm sorry." Jane's tone changed. "As for me, I'm used to it. If you don't mind, I'm going on. I don't admit the possibility of anyone ever having been here before us. I mean to be an explorer. Were there any celebrated women explorers?"

"Not many, I'm afraid. There's one in Chicago who goes across Africa once in a while."

"Well, I'm going to explore. You watch me!" Jane

"Look at That Ledge!" Jane Pointed to the Right

laughed as she marched away into the brush. Soon enough she was to discover that her statement that no one had been here before them was not well founded.

Left to herself, Greta wandered back to camp, found a few live coals which she fanned into flame, added fresh fuel to the fire, and sat down wearily.

The morning had been chilly. A cold wind swept in from black waters. But now the sun was up. Gentle breezes, like fairies' wings, brushed her cheeks. On a level space beneath her, thimbleberry blossoms lay like a blanket of snow. Away to the right a rocky slope flamed all golden with wild tiger lilies.

"It—it's like a fire," she told herself, gazing into her own half-burned-out campfire.

There is something about an open fire that takes us back and back to days we have never truly known at all, the days of our pioneer ancestors.

To Greta on this particular morning the crackle of the fire seemed a call from some long-forgotten past.

Their camp lay within the shadow of a great rock. The fire whispered of good fellowship and cheer. The day before had been a long one. Her muscles were still stiff from that long tramp. As she sat there gazing into the narrow fiery chasm made by half-burned logs, she began to daydream and maybe even doze a bit.

As her eyes narrowed it seemed to her that the fiery chasm expanded until at last it was so high she might step inside if she willed to do so.

"So warm! So bright! So cheery!" she whispered. "One might—"

But what was this? With a startled scream she sprang to her feet.

"Jane! It was Jane!" she cried aloud.

Then, coming into full possession of her faculties, she stood and stared.

At that moment, as if the show were ended, the bits of burning wood crumbled into a heap. The chasm of fire was no more.

But what had she seen there? It was strange. She had seen quite plainly there at the center of the fiery circle the form of her companion, Jane.

"Jane." She said the word softly. "Of course she was not there; not even her image was there. And yet—

"I wonder if it is truly possible to hear another think when she is far away? There are cases on record when this has seemed to be true. Mental telepathy they call it.

"I wonder if that vision could have been a warning?

"This place—" she shuddered. "It haunts me. Let me get out into the sunlight!

"Surely," she told herself soberly, "if we may not

listen to our friends' thoughts when they are far away, at least God can whisper them in our ears. With Him all things are possible. I must try to find Jane. I am afraid she may be in trouble."

With that she walked some distance along the slope and at last vanished down a narrow moose trail that passed between two black old spruce trees.

Early that same morning Bihari and his band, with Petite Jeanne in their midst, were having their breakfast coffee on deck, when a yellow-haired youth came rowing alongside in a roughly-made fishing boat. Two small children rode in the stern.

"Swen!" Jeanne cried joyously. "So that *is* your lighthouse! That is your home!"

"Yes," Swen grinned broadly. "Anyway, I thought it was. Since—"

"But Swen!" Jeanne broke in, "you never told me you were married. What beautiful children!"

The children beamed up at her. But not Swen. He was blushing from ear to ear.

"Children!" he exclaimed. "My children! I am but eighteen. What could you think? They are not my children. They are my brother's. Their home is in the cabin by the lighthouse. And my home—" He hesitated, looking from face to face as if trying to read something there. "The lighthouse, it is my home. But someone, it seems, wants to tear it up.

What can I think?

"When I came home last night," he rushed on, "all is strange. The doorstep is broken. My bench by the door, it is tipped over. There are bits of cloth everywhere. And my axe, it is thrown on the ground. In the tower it is no better. The trap door, it is broken, stones are thrown down and my rope, it is gone."

For a moment, when he had finished, Jeanne stared at him. Then, as in a dream, she murmured. "It was the bear. He got away yesterday and went to shore. I'm so sorry he got into your house."

"No," said Swen, "it was not the bear."

"Come up and have a cup of coffee," said Jeanne. She had recovered some of her composure. "Bring those beautiful children. We will have a romp with the bear. And then, then I will help you solve your riddle."

She laughed a merry laugh.

CHAPTER EIGHTEEN

THE ANCIENT MINE

And what of Jane? For one thing, she had made a marvelous discovery.

After leaving her companion, she had wandered for two hours along Greenstone Ridge. Here she paused to examine the surface of a greenish wall of rock. There she drew a chisel and small hammer from her pocket to drill away on a spot of green. And now, with no thought of rock or greenstone treasure, head down, deep in thought, she wandered along some moose trail.

As she walked along she struck her foot against some solid object and all but fell forward on her face.

"What—what was that?" She turned about. "Only a rock. And—and yet—"

She bent over to look more closely. An exclamation of joy escaped her lips.

"A hammer! An Indian hammer!"

At once she was down on her knees, tearing away at the thick moss that on Isle Royale hides many a secret.

That the history of this interesting island goes far back of the time when the first white trader saw it, she well knew.

Back in the dim past Indian tribes fought many a bloody battle over the copper of this strange island. Here, as we have said before, copper in solid masses might be found close to the surface. Rich indeed was the tribe that possessed copper for knives, beads, spear points, and arrowheads.

"I'll find something more before I leave," Jane told herself.

As she looked at the surface she had bared she stared in surprise. She had uncovered a mass of charcoal.

"And yet there can have been no forest fire." She looked at the great two-foot-thick trunk of a spruce tree.

"An Indian mine!" she exclaimed. "They built a fire on the surface, then dragged it away to break hot rock with these stone hammers."

She scraped away the charcoal with a sharp stick. As she did so something gave forth a low metallic clink.

"No, not a coin, but a knife," she whispered. "An ancient copper knife! How perfect!" It was indeed a far more perfect specimen than the one she had found on the camping ground. She held the thin blade to the light. Dating back beyond the days of the white man, it held for her an indescribable charm.

"The whole island is a treasure house. I'll find another." Once more she prodded away at the moss and charcoal. Not a second knife, but a spear point greeted her excited vision.

She widened her search. Prying away at a deep bed of moss, she tore it away in a yard-square chunk. And there beneath it, grinning and horrible, was a skull.

At that instant something stirred in the brush above her. With a startled scream she whirled about, took one step backward, lost her balance and plunged downward.

She had gone over the ridge. For an instant her heart was in her mouth; the next she realized that the slope, which was not too steep, ended in a second narrow plateau.

Struggling to break her downward plunge, she grasped at a branch. The branch snapped off. She snatched at a trailing vine, but that too broke under her weight.

Just when she was waiting the final bump that should announce her arrival at the bottom, she dropped a surprising distance straight down, glanced to the right, slid some twenty feet, then dropped again to land with such a rude shock that for a moment she lay there utterly oblivious to her strange surroundings.

When at last she came to, and strove to discover

Jane Grasped a Branch as She Plunged Downward

what had happened, she found herself in a place of almost complete darkness. Only straight above her, at what seemed an incredible distance, a narrow crack of light shone.

She rose stiffly to feel of her bruises. "None of them are fatal, I guess." She tried to face the situation with a smile.

"I don't know where I am, but I'll not stay here long."

Had she believed in imps she might have fancied one saying: "Oh, won't you?"

As she stretched her hands above her head to feel for some means of drawing herself up, she found nothing but solid rock.

For the first time she was truly startled. Where was she? How was she to escape?

Thrusting a hand in her pocket, she drew out a box of safety matches. Having lighted one, she looked about her. By the yellow light she discovered several facts. This place had been made by men. Holes had been drilled in the rock. The rock had been blasted away. At her feet were bits of greenish rock. This, she found, was not rock, but pieces of pure copper.

"An abandoned copper mine! A white man's mine!" Her heart sank. Not one of these mines had been worked for forty years.

"I've got to get out of here some way," she said,

looking about.

She studied the rocky surface about her. "Might get a good foothold here and—"

The match burned out. She lit another. "Could get a handhold there, and there!"

She doubted her ability to make this perilous ascent. She had been fortunate to escape with no broken bones. Next time it was very possible she might not fare as well.

"I might scream. There's no harm in that, and someone might hear me."

She screamed at the top of her voice and at once felt better.

When, however, after a half hour's attempt at scaling the rocky wall, she found herself still at the bottom of the mine with only fresh bruises to show for her trouble, she was near to despair.

Then a curious thing happened. Some object came bumping down the wall, which at the upper edge was not steep.

"It's a rock that broke loose." She dodged. "Or some pebbles some animal dislodged while going along the trail."

The thing struck her on the head. It was no rock. It was soft.

Gropingly she felt for and found it.

"Leather," she whispered. "Some little leather-covered book."

Lighting a match, she examined the little black book. She had just opened this blank book and was looking at a picture between the pages, when of a sudden her heart stood still.

Something was coming down the wall, not bumping, but gliding, slowly dodging the trees and bushes as though it were guided.

As she waited breathless, her match burned her fingers. And still there came that scraping, gliding sound. Her match sputtered out. She was in the dark.

"Th—there it is," she breathed as she pressed back against the wall and watched the thing slithering down the rock. "It—it's a snake! A big snake!"

She was ready to scream with fright when the real nature of that gliding thing came to her.

"It's a rope! A rope!" she exclaimed in a hoarse whisper. Then—

"Greta! Greta! Are you there?"

There was no answer. The rope had ceased to glide. It hung invitingly before her. All was still as the grave.

Her heart thumped madly. Who was up there? Had the mystery man of Greenstone Ridge come to her aid? Who was he? What was he like? Why did he stay on the ridge?

Suddenly she found herself more afraid than before.

"I don't want to touch that rope." Her whisper ended in tremor. "I—I'm afraid. I don't know who is at the other end of it. But I must get out of this old mine some way."

CHAPTER NINETEEN

MYSTERY FROM THE SKY

Petite Jeanne loved children. She thought that
Nelse and Freda, the tots who had come with Swen,
dressed in their quaint home-made garments, were
about the most fascinating creatures she had seen
in all the wide world. While Swen enjoyed his coffee
and told Bihari in an excited manner of what had
happened at his house during his absence on the
evening before, she led her two young friends to
the prow of the boat where the bear, like a huge
dog, lay sprawled out on the deck.

Seeing their eyes open big with wonder and fear,
she commanded the bear to get to his feet, and led
him across the deck in a clumsy dance.

In less time than it takes to tell it, they were whirling about in a ring-around-a-rosy, Nelse and Freda,
Jeanne and the big brown bear.

"Do you stay here all through the cold winter?"
she asked, when at last, quite exhausted, they
dropped in a pile on the deck.

"Oh, yes," Nelse said cheerfully. "There is great
fun! Snow for forts, ice for sliding. Winter is grand!"

"But there is no school!" she protested.

They did not seem very sorry about this, but

158

Jeanne, recalling Swen's desire for a boat that more money might be made by fishing and that these little ones might go to the mainland where there were schools, wished harder than ever that Jane's dream of finding a barrel of gold might come true.

"A barrel of gold!" she murmured. "What a lot of gold that must be!"

She thought of her castle in France and almost wished she could have spent it for these bright-eyed little ones.

"But then," she sighed, "one cannot spend a castle anyway. And there is Great-Aunt Minyon who would not allow me to spend a penny of it, even if it were possible. No! No! We must find our barrel of gold!"

All this time there remained in the back of the little French girl's head a question. "What did Swen mean when he said his doorstep had been broken, his bench overturned, and bits of cloth scattered before his door? Just what he said, to be sure.

"And the bear!" she whispered. "He was on shore a long time. What did he do?"

To these questions she was destined to find no certain answer. When she had told Swen her part of the story and together they had searched the vicinity of Swen's home for some clue as to the whereabouts of the head hunter, they could arrive at no definite conclusions regarding any part of the mysterious affair.

"One thing is sure," Swen declared at last. "We will not make him happy if he comes about our place again! We do not wish our moose killed, nor the good people who visit our island disturbed."

It did not seem probable that the man would return to this spot. "But where will we hear of him next?" Jeanne's brow wrinkled. She thought of her two good pals up there somewhere on the ridge, then of their deserted home, the wreck.

"Does he belong to that black schooner with the diver on board?" she asked herself. She did not think so. "But what of that schooner?"

She decided in the end to abandon the task of solving mysteries and to give herself over, for the time, to the wild, care-free life of Bihari and his band. For all that, as the *Ship of Joy*, riding the long sweeping waves that follow every storm, went plowing its way out of Rock Harbor and into the open lake, this little French girl sat upon the deck, staring at the sky. Her eyes were seeing things in the clouds.

"A barrel of gold!" she whispered. Then, in a hoarse exclamation, "How absurd! And yet, one can dream."

In the meantime Greta, impelled by memory of a strange vision seen in the cavern of fire, had started out in search of her companion. She found little to

Jeanne Dreamed of the Barrel of Gold

guide her on her way. Jane had gone away to the right of their camp. This much she knew; nothing more.

She had not proceeded far before she discovered that the narrow plateau was a bewildering labyrinth of trees, bushes, and rocks. More than this, its surface was as irregular as the face of the deep in time of storm. Here it rose steep as a stairway, there sloped away to end in a stretch flat as a floor.

"I'll never find her in such a place," Greta grumbled.

"Jane!" she shouted. "Jane!"

There was no answer save the long-drawn whistle of a bird.

The silence and loneliness of the place began to oppress her. The memory of that scream in the night remained in her mind as something distinct, sinister.

"Who could that have been?" she asked herself with a shudder. "Why did they scream? What could have happened?"

Her mind was filled with bits of stories of crimes committed in secret places.

"It's absurd!" She paused to stamp her foot. "Nothing of importance will come of it. Mysteries fade before the light of day. The sun is shining. Why do I shudder? And for that matter, why am I here at all? A vision brought me here, a dream dreamed out by the fire. I—"

She broke off short to listen. Faint and from far away there came the drone of an airplane motor.

"The amphibian from Houghton," she told herself. "Wonder if it will come near?"

Every day in summer, sometimes two or three times a day, this bi-motored plane brought passengers and sightseers to Isle Royale. The moose feeding on grass on the shores of inland lakes had learned to glance up at its approach, then go on with their feeding. They paid no more attention to it than they paid to a hawk flying over the island.

Greta thought little of an airplane's approach. Indeed, she had all but forgotten it when, as she reached a rocky space quite devoid of trees and found herself in a position to look down upon another plateau that lay some two hundred feet below, she was made doubly conscious of its presence.

"Why it—it's not the bi-motor at all!" she exclaimed. "It's some strange plane, all white, and it —it's landing!"

Instinctively she drew back into the shadow.

On the surface of that other plateau she discovered a narrow lake, little more than a pond in size, but doubtlessly quite deep. It was on this lake that the plane was about to land. Having circled twice, it came swooping down to touch the water gently, gracefully as some wild migrating bird.

"Wonderful!" she murmured in admiration.

But that was not all. She had assumed for the moment that this was but a chance landing, caused perhaps by motor trouble. That it was not she was soon enough to know, for the plane taxied toward a large clump of dark spruce trees. And to the girl's astonishment a narrow boat, painted the color of the water, stole out from that shore to at last glide alongside the now motionless plane.

"Sol—solitude!" she murmured. "No one up here. They told us that. And now look! There must be a settlement. What—"

Something strange was going on down there. She crawled back among the pine needles and hid herself in some bushes. Someone was being lifted out of the plane and into the boat. Now the boat with its apparently helpless burden was pulling for the shore. Studying this shore for a space of seconds, she thought she made out some sort of lodge there among the trees.

Her heart pounded painfully. What was this? A kidnaping? A murder? Strange doings! It was a curious sort of place these people had chosen for all this!

She did not wait to see more. Gliding about the pine tree, she headed straight for her own camp; nor did she pause till the white of their small tent showed through the trees.

At the very moment Greta sighted their tent, Jane

stood contemplating the rope that had so miracu-
lously come to her aid.

"Greta!" she called once more, this time softly.
There was no answer.

"It couldn't be Greta." She experienced a wild
flutter at her heart. "We have no rope like that. But
who can it be?"

"There's somebody waiting for you up there."
The words of the young fisherman came back to her,
this time with a force that carried conviction.

"Someone up here," she murmured, "but who,
and why? What can that person be like?"

Recalling the face in the little book, she drew the
book again from her pocket, struck a match, then
peered at the picture.

A youngish face topped by a mass of almost white
hair seemed to smile at her from the book.

"A man!" She caught her breath. "He's handsome. I've never seen him around the island. I
wonder who he is!"

Then realizing that she might be seen in that
circle of yellow light, she snuffed out the match,
snapped the book shut, then stood at attention,
listening.

Aside from the long-drawn whistle of some small
bird and the sighing of the breeze through the pines,
no sound reached her ears.

"Well," she sighed, "there's no good in delay."

Putting her hand to the rope, she tested it. "Solid! Solid as the rock itself. Now! Up I go!"

Jane was no weakling. Boating, swimming, hiking in summer, skating and skiing in winter kept her ever at her best.

She did not stop to think about the climb. She gripped the rope, took a deep breath and started to climb hand over hand up the rope. Having scaled the steep portion, she paused for a second breath, then raced upward to find—

"No—no one here!" she breathed as her keen eyes took in every detail, rock, bush, and tree.

"Someone heard me call, came to my aid, then vanished. How—how weird!"

As if possessed by the idea that the place might be haunted, and leaving the rope as it hung, she quickly left the spot and ran down the moose trail to their camp. How good the sight of that little white tent was when she spied it through the trees!

"Where—where have you been?" Greta demanded as Jane at last hurried into camp and threw herself on the ground beside the fire. "Did something happen to you?"

Jane stared at her speechless. For a full moment she could not speak. When she found her voice she blurted out:

"Do you mean to tell me you lowered that rope, then bolted?"

"What rope?" Greta stared.

"The rope in the old mine."

"What mine?"

Jane burst out laughing. "What a world! You ask me if I have been in danger. I have. But, after all, you seem to know nothing of it. How—how does that happen?" She drew herself up closer to a place before the freshly-kindled fire.

"I dreamed it, I guess," Greta replied slowly. "But please do tell me about it."

"I will. But first—" Jane drew the small blank book from her pocket, opened it to the picture, then asked quietly, "Did you ever see him before?"

"Why, yes, I—" Greta's face was a study. "Jane, where *did* you get that?"

"It came tumbling down into the mine."

There was a touch of something akin to awe in Greta's voice as she said hoarsely, "That is a picture of the most wonderful musician I have ever heard. He plays the violin with a touch almost divine."

"The violin!"

"Yes. But, Jane—" Greta leaned forward eagerly. "Tell me all about it. Tell me what happened to you!"

When Jane had told her story Greta sat for a long time staring at the fire. When at last she spoke it was in a subdued and mellow tone. "That," she said, pointing to the little book that lay open before them, "is the picture of Percy O'Hara.

"It was more than three years ago that I heard him play. It happened that I was with one of his personal friends. After the concert I was introduced to him. Can you imagine?" Her laugh was low and melodious. "I actually shook hands with him, the truly great O'Hara.

"I'm afraid I was a bit romantic. I was young. He became my hero in a way. I tried to keep track of his triumphs. But quite suddenly his triumphs ceased. I heard nothing about him. There was a rumor that he had disappeared. What do you think could have happened? Surely one who had entranced thousands with his music would not voluntarily allow himself to be lost—lost from the world that loves him!"

"Something terrible may have happened to him." Jane was staring at the fire. "Terrible things do happen these days."

"And this picture?" Greta whispered. "Where did it come from?"

"It probably belongs to some ardent admirer like yourself."

"But listen, Jane—" Greta's lips tightened, a fresh light shone in her face. "I too have had an adventure, discovered a mystery. There is a narrow lake off there to the right and below us. A monoplane landed there today. Someone was lifted from the plane into a boat. They rowed to the shore where

"After the Concert I Was Introduced to Him."

there is some sort of lodge. What can that mean?"

"As far as we are concerned," Jane responded soberly, "it seems to mean that we should strike our
tent and descend to less inhabited regions where we
can enjoy ourselves in peace."

"And leave those people to go on with their evil
deeds?"

"How do you know they are evil?"

"Who would hide away up here if their purposes
were lawful? Think, Jane! They may be kidnapers!
That person may be a victim!"

"Yes," exclaimed Jane, springing to her feet, "and
they may be law-abiding citizens! Come, you have
given me the creeps. Besides, I'm starving. You get
some bacon frying while I start the coffee. We'll eat.
That will brighten our horizon."

The rest of the day the girls spent about their
camp. They did not venture far away, but read,
talked about the mysteries and dozed. They wondered where Jeanne was and what she was doing.
What was happening on the *Pilgrim?* Had the black
schooner and the diver returned? Had they ran-
sacked the hold of the ship? What had they found?
Surely, in the last few days enough had happened
to give the girls plenty to talk about.

Nine o'clock came. Seated before a fire of brightly
gleaming coals, their cozy bed of blankets and balsam boughs awaiting them, the two girls forgot the

mysteries and adventures of the day to sit and talk, as young people will, of home, of friends, of hopes and fears, and of the future that stretches on and on before them like a golden pathway. They were deep in this whispered reverie when, gripping her companion's arm, Greta exclaimed, "There it is again!"

A wild, piercing, blood-curdling scream had rent the air of night.

"Wha—what can it be?" As if for protection the slim girl threw herself into the arms of her companion.

"It's no loon!" Jane measured her words. "It's some human being in distress."

"I told you!" Greta shuddered.

"We should go to their aid."

"But just two girls! What could we do? We—"

"Listen!" Jane touched Greta's lips. From afar, as on that other night, there came, wafted in faint and glorious tones, the whisper of a violin.

"I'll tell you!" Greta sprang to her feet. "That man playing the violin has nothing to do with this other affair. He couldn't possibly, or how could he play so divinely?"

"He couldn't. He must be a friend of Percy O'Hara or he wouldn't have had his picture. He is interested in others or he would not have lowered that rope to me. We must hunt him out and make him help us."

"But how do you know it is a man? Why not a girl, or two girls like ourselves?" Greta doubted.

"It must be a man; it just must be! Come!" Jane pulled her companion to her feet. "Come, we will follow the sound of the phantom violin."

Jane led the way. It was strange, this following a sound into the night. More than once Greta found herself in the grip of an almost irresistible desire to turn back; yet always that cry of terror seemed to ring in her ears and she whispered: "We must go on!"

The trail they followed was one made by wild creatures. And night is their time for being abroad. Now as they pressed forward they caught the sound of some wolf or lynx sneaking away into the brush. Would they always flee or would one someday turn on them and attack them? Greta shuddered as she asked the question.

From time to time they paused to listen for those silver notes of the phantom violin. "It's growing louder," Jane whispered on each occasion

Once, after they had remained motionless for some time, she said with an air of certainty, "It comes from over the ridge."

Soon after that they took a side trail and began to climb. This path was steep, almost straight up the cliff. More than once Greta caught her breath sharply as her foot slipped. Jane struggled steadily upward until with a deep sigh she exclaimed, "There!"

She said no more. For a space of seconds the violin had been silent. Now, as the music burst once more upon their ears, it seemed almost upon them.

"A—a little farther." The slender girl gripped Jane's arm until it hurt. "It's not far away now."

Just then the moon went under a cloud.

"Look!" Greta whispered in an awed tone. "Look! What is that?"

Before them, just how far away they could not tell, shone what appeared to be innumerable pairs of eyes.

"Green eyes!" Greta whispered.

The next moment her voice rose in a note of sheer terror.

"Jane! Jane! Where are you?" There was no answer. Jane had vanished into the night.

CHAPTER TWENTY

AID FROM THE UNKNOWN

As Greta called for the second time, "Jane! Jane! Where are you?" an answer came floating up to her from the crevice next to the path.

"Here! Down below. I—I'm coming up." There was a suggestion of suppressed pain in Jane's voice. "Wait, you wait there."

Greta had never found waiting easy. To wait now, with a hundred green eyes focused upon her was all but impossible. And yet, what more was to be done? Jane, when she fell down the hillside in the dark, had taken the flashlight with her. And the darkness all about was intense. Without willing it, Greta again and again fixed her eyes on those small glowing orbs of green. "If I only knew!" she whispered, and again, "If I only knew what those were!"

She heard her companion's panting breath as she struggled up the uncertain slope. "She must be half way up," she whispered finally.

There came the sound of tumbling rocks. "She—she slipped!" Catching her breath, she waited. Yes, yes. she was climbing again.

And then as she was about to despair, a bulk loomed beside her, a strong arm encircled her.

"Greta," a voice whispered, "I've sprained my ankle, not too badly. The flashlight is broken. We must try to find our way back to our camp in the dark."

Feeling their way along the narrow path, the girls made their way in the direction from which they had come. Often they tripped and almost fell over stones and branches. Several times Jane had to sit down and rest her painful ankle.

Two hours of groping and stumbling, with many a fall, two hours of fighting vines and brambles; then the dull glow of their burned-out campfire greeted their eyes.

"Home!" Jane breathed. "Home!" And to this girl at that hour the humble six-foot-square tent, which they had set up that evening, was just that— nothing less.

It was Jane who could not sleep that night. The throbbing pain in the sprained ankle defied rest. The strange events of that day and those that had gone before had at last broken through her staunch reserve and entered her inner consciousness.

"Sleep!" she exclaimed at last in a hoarse whisper. "Who can sleep?"

Strangely enough, at that moment in a little cabin at Chippewa Harbor, Vincent Stearns, the young newspaper photographer who had given Greta the white flares, lay on his cot looking away at the moon and wondering in a vague sort of way what was happening to his dark-eyed friend up there on Greenstone Ridge.

"I hope she finds some rare greenstones," he said to the moon. "I hope she is finding some happy adventure.

"And if that girl's adventures are not happy ones, there will come the white flare in the night.

"The white flare." He found himself wishing against the will of his better self that he might catch the gleam of that white light against the skyline. "What an adventure!" he murmured. "Racing away to Lake Ritchie, paddling like mad, then struggling up the ridge in the night to find—"

Well, what would he find? What did he expect to find? He did not know. Yet something seemed to tell him that perhaps at some unearthly hour the light of the flare would send its bright call for help against the sky.

Having given up thoughts of sleep, Jane was going over in her mind everything that had happened that day.

"The hydroplane," she thought. "Who can be coming up here to hide away on the shore of that narrow lake? And why?

"How simple it is after all, coming up here in a

"What an Adventure! To Race Across the Lake!"

plane without attracting attention! The plane from Houghton comes and goes at all hours. The people at Rock Harbor hear it. If it does not land at their door, they say, 'It has gone to Tobin's Harbor or Belle Isle.' The folks at Tobin's Harbor and Belle Isle think it has gone to Rock Harbor. The strange plane may come and go up here as its pilot wishes, and no one will be the wiser.

"After all," she sighed, "we are not officers of the law. It's really not our affair. And yet I wish I knew what it was doing here."

She was thinking of the scream Greta had heard, and of the apparently helpless person carried to a boat and then to land, and after that of the scream they had both heard in the night.

"Life," she told herself, "all human life is so precious that it is the duty of all to protect those who are in danger.

"Probably it is nothing very terrible," she assured herself. "Nothing to be afraid of. We—"

She broke her thoughts off to lean forward and listen intently. Had she caught some sound from without, the snapping of a twig perhaps, or the rustle of some curious animal prowling among the bushes looking for a midnight meal?

"It's probably some animal," she told herself sleepily.

Not satisfied with this, she opened the flaps of the

tent and peered into the moonlight.

The moon was high. The silence was uncanny. Every object—trees, bushes, rocks—stood out like pictures in fairyland. Shadows were deep wells of darkness.

Some ten feet from their tent was a large flat rock, their table they called it. This stood full in the moonlight. That they had left nothing on this table Jane knew right well. She had washed it clean with a canvas bucket full of water from a spring. But there seemed to be something there now. She was sure she saw something.

She rubbed her eyes to look again. No, she was not mistaken. Two objects rested on that rock, one was white as snow, the other was dark and gleamed in the moonlight.

"Well," she sighed, "I'll have to see what it is."

Creeping from the warm blankets, she stepped on the cold, damp ground. "Oo!" she shuddered. The next instant her hands closed on the mysterious objects.

"How—how strange!" She shuddered again, but not from the cold, then beat a hasty retreat back to her bed.

Inside the tent, she turned the objects over in her hands. One was a large roll of bandages, the other a bottle of liniment.

"Who—" she whispered, "who could that have

been?"

The answer came to her instantly. "The one who lowered the rope into the copper mine. And, perhaps, the one who plays the violin so gloriously. And who is he?" Here was a question she could not answer.

" 'Take, eat,' " she whispered the words of a half forgotten poem.

" 'Take, eat,' he said, 'and be content.
        These fishes in your stead were sent
    By him who sent the tangled ram
        To spare the child of Abraham!' "

At that she rubbed the liniment over her swollen ankle vigorously, bound it tightly, then crept beneath the blankets once more.

Though the bandage relieved her somewhat, she was still conscious of pain. Our waking thoughts as well as our dreams are often inspired by physical sensations. Pain awakens within us a longing for some spot where we have known perfect peace. To Jane, at the moment, this meant the deck of the unfortunate *Pilgrim*. There, with the waves lapping the old ship's sides, the gentle breezes whispering and the gulls soaring high, she had found peace and quiet.

As she allowed her mind to drift back to those blissful days, she was tempted to wish that she and the slender, dark-eyed Greta at her side had never set foot on Greenstone Ridge.

"And yet—" she whispered. The words of some great prophet came to her. " 'There is a destiny that shapes our ends, rough-hew them how we may.'

"It was written in the stars that we should be here," she told herself. "And, being here, we shall do what we can for those who are nearest us.

"But we shall go back to the wreck."

She thought of the narrow camping grounds on the shores of Duncan's Bay. "There is treasure hidden there," she told herself. "How can it be otherwise? It is the only bit of level land on that side of Blake's Point. Countless generations of men have camped there. We will go back there and dig deep and see what we can find."

"And when I am weary of digging—" she laughed a low laugh, "I'll go back and get that monster of a pike. I'll go all by myself. And will I land him? Just you wait!"

A shadow passed over her brow as she thought of the head hunter. "Terrible man! Where can he be now?"

She thought of the strange black schooner with a deep-sea diver on board. "There is some treasure on that old ship. When I'm back I'll try diving to see what's there. It might be more important than the wreckers, who stripped the ship, knew.

"All we need," she whispered dreamily as the

drugging odor of balsam and the silence of night crept over her, "all we need is a barrel of gold. One barrel of—"

She did not finish. She had fallen asleep.

CHAPTER TWENTY-ONE

A SONG FROM THE TREETOPS

Greta Clara Bronson was by nature a musician, an artist, a person of temperament. The dawn of another day found her in no mood for seeking adventure. The troubles of others, if indeed there were troubled ones in these hills, seemed far away.

Having made sure that her companion's sprained ankle was not a matter of serious consequence, she found herself ready for a day of rest and thought; not serious thought, but the dreamy sort that leads one's mind, like a drifting cobweb, into unknown lands.

All the long forenoon she lay upon a bed of moss in the sun. At times she dreamed of her home and mother. This seemed very far away. Would she return to it all? Surely. " 'When the frost is on the pumpkin,' " she whispered. Looking up at the sun, she smiled.

For an hour she dreamed of the wreck and of the shady shores of Duncan's Bay. "Dizzy," she whispered, "I wonder where he is?" Before leaving the wreck, they had set their pet loon free. He seemed quite able to care for himself. "Probably he's gone ashore and has laughed his head off at some crazy loon that looks just like him," she chuckled.

"But Jeanne?" Greta asked herself. "Is she truly happy with those queer gypsy people? How strange it seems!"

Yes, Jeanne was happy with "those queer people." Having, as of old, forgotten all thought of the morrow, she had in true gypsy fashion thrown herself with abandon into the joys of each new day.

At Chippewa Harbor there were a few small cabins and many tents. The visitors showered silver down upon her tambourine when her dance with the bear was over. "Frank, joyous, kindly people, these Americans," she thought. "What a glorious land!"

And yet her keenest joy came when, after climbing a ridge, she came at last upon a lake three miles long, a mile wide, where there was no one. "Dark forests, darker water, wild animals, wild birds, and deep, glorious silence," she whispered to the companion at her side. "How grand to pitch a tent on these shores and live here many long days!"

So the *Ship of Joy* made its way slowly along the shores of Isle Royale, and still the dark-eyed Greta sat far up on that ridge dreaming the hours away.

After lunch Greta declared her intention of going out to play for the birds.

Tucking her violin under her arm, she wandered

away up the ridge. At the summit, somewhat to her surprise, she found a hard-beaten trail. Traveling here with ease, she wandered on and on until with a little start she found herself recognizing a certain jagged rock formation.

"I must have been here before." She stopped dead in her tracks. "I have! Last night!"

Should she turn back? Where were the green eyes?

"Green eyes do not shine in the day!" she laughed a little. "Ghosts, witches, green eyes, they all vanish at dawn."

Seating herself on a moss-covered rock, she began thrumming the strings of her violin. Then she sent out some little plaintive snatches of song.

She paused to lean far forward, intent, alert, expectant. Yes, there it was. A bird had answered.

After listening, she imitated his call. Then she listened again.

"Yes, yes, my little one!" Her heart warmed to the tiny whistler of Greenstone Ridge. "He's coming closer."

Once more she repeated his song. This time there were two replies, one near and one far away. Soon it seemed the bushes, the trees, the very air was filled with little gray and brown songsters. Thrilled by this unique experience, she forgot both time and place as she proceeded to charm her tiny listeners.

Place was brought back to her with startling force.

Some great creature came thrashing through the brush.

With a low cry, Greta gripped her precious violin and sprang for the nearest tree.

Just in time she was, for a bull moose charged full upon the spot where she had been. Why he charged will remain a mystery. Perhaps he did not like music. Enough that he was here; and here, beyond a shadow of a doubt, he meant to stay.

Having spent a full ten minutes sharpening his jagged antlers on a dead cottonwood tree, he marched up to Greta's fir tree, leaned his full weight against it, then gave forth a most terrifying roar. Finding the tree quite solid and alive, he dropped with a grunt on the bed of moss at the foot of the tree and pretended at last to fall asleep.

"Our next number," Greta said quite soberly, "will be a cradle song entitled 'When Father Moose Goes to Sleep.' "

The thing she played, perched there on a limb, was not that at all, but an exquisite fantasy written after some all-but-forgotten folk song of the gypsies.

Caught by the charm of it, she played it over and over.

Then, to her astonishment, as the notes faded away and she rested there among the branches, someone took up her song.

"A violin!" she whispered. "The phantom violin!

"What Are You Doing Up There?" a Pleasant Voice Asked

And so close at hand!"

The effect, there in the gathering twilight, was like a touch of magic.

The silence that followed the stranger's last note was most profound, so perfect that the flutter of a small bird's wings might be heard ten yards away. Charmed by this little touch of the dramatic, Greta forgot that she was perched in a tree, that a monstrous moose lay at the foot of that tree, and that darkness was falling. Lips parted, ears strained, she waited for one more note from that magic violin.

It did not come. Instead she heard a pleasant voice say, "What are you doing up there?"

"Quiet!" she warned. "There is a moose at the foot of the tree."

"Oh ho! That's it!" There came a mellow laugh. "Some bluffing old moose has you treed. Watch me get rid of him!"

Next instant an ear-splitting shout rent the night air.

There came a terrific thumping at the foot of her tree, followed by a sound of crashing of bushes that rapidly diminished in the distance.

"He's gone," the voice called up to her. "Come down!"

A brief scramble, then she found herself looking into a smiling face. The face was framed by a bushy mass of gray hair; yet the face was young. It was the face of the picture in that little blank book Jane had found in the mine.

"Per—Percy O'Hara!" Her lips could scarcely frame the words.

"You—" the man stepped back. "How did you know me?"

"I've always known you, at—at least for a very long time. But why are you here?"

"That," he smiled, a strange smile, "that, dear child, is a long story."

"A child," said Greta smilingly, "likes to hear stories."

"Is it not enough," he laughed a low laugh, "that I have saved you from a wild and ferocious beast who, joking aside, would have slept right there all night? And must I tell you a story besides?"

"Perhaps," said the girl soberly, "you have more to gain by telling me the story than I have by listening."

A frown gathered on his brow. She shuddered in fear. Had she displeased him? Yet again the ready smile returned.

"Stories," he said quietly, "must be told in just the right setting. This is not the time. Another day perhaps. Not now. I—"

He broke off short. His face took on a look of horror. "Wha—what was that?"

Up from the depths below, where darkness was

falling among the black fir trees, rising like a siren, had come one long, piercing scream.

Then silence and falling darkness settled over them like a shroud.

CHAPTER TWENTY-TWO

THE WHITE FLARE

"That scream! What was it?" The figure of Percy O'Hara had suddenly grown tense. In the gathering darkness he seemed cast in bronze.

To the slim girl, who but the moment before had thought of this marvelous violinist as a phantom, the whole thing seemed unreal. "Have you never heard it before?" she asked with a voice that trembled.

"Heard that scream before?" He stared at her.

"I heard it two nights ago. But that was late, near midnight," she said. "There are people down below by a narrow lake. They come and go in an airplane. There's a lodge of some sort and a small rowboat. They carried someone into the lodge, someone who was helpless, crippled or bound. I could not tell."

"You know all this, you who have been here so short a time?"

"Yes."

"I knew that someone came and went over there." He spoke slowly. "But I—you see I've wanted to be alone. If you go about spying on others you're likely to be found out yourself. I did not hear the scream at midnight. I must have been sound asleep. But we must do something. We—"

"Look!" The girl gripped his arm impulsively. "Look! It's Jane! The white flare!"

Even as she spoke the night shadows were banished and every smallest shrub and bush stood out as in the light of day.

"Come!" she cried. "We must go! It is Jane. That is a signal, a sign of danger. But—" her tone changed, "how could that be a signal? I never told her about the white flares. They were given to me as a signal to be used in case of danger."

"A signal to whom?"

"Vincent Stearns," she replied, her voice all atremble. "He will come. Something terrible has happened! We must hurry!"

"In just one moment. I will be back. Don't go without me. I know a short trail. We'll be there at once." Her new-found friend disappeared into the night.

At once the girl's mind was awhirl with questions. So this was the phantom. Why had this wonderful musician hidden himself away here on Isle Royale? Had he committed some grave crime? It was unthinkable. And yet, why was he here? Would she ever know?

Then her thoughts took another turn. Who had screamed? Why had Jane lighted the white flare? Because of the scream? She would hardly do that, and besides, she did not know of the flares.

"Oh why did we come here?" Greta said the words aloud.

Then turning instinctively, she looked to see if Percy O'Hara might have heard.

Percy O'Hara was not to be seen. That which met her gaze set her knees trembling afresh. Once again she was looking into what appeared to be a hundred pairs of green and gleaming eyes.

"Here we are!" She started violently.

Percy O'Hara was at her side. "We'll go this way. Follow the ridge. I'll lead the way." Without another word he marched straight ahead, leaving her to follow.

He walked unerringly as some wild creature of the forest, straight to the small tent beside the big flat rock.

They found Jane quite unharmed, but in a state of great agitation. "Oh, Greta!" she exclaimed. Then, catching sight of Percy O'Hara, broke off short to stare.

"Wha—what happened?" Greta panted. "This is Mr. O'Hara. Tell me what happened!"

"Nothing happened—that is, nothing much. Did you hear that scream?"

"Yes. We—"

"Well, I heard it and came dashing from the tent. My foot struck something and sent it bounding into

the fire. Before I could grab it, there came a blind-
ing white flare. I jumped back just in time to save
myself. And now—"

"And now," Greta broke in, "Vincent Stearns
will come all the way up the ridge from—from wherever he is. He—he'll bring others, like as not, to—to
save us from some—something terrible. Oh!" she
fairly wailed, "that's what one gets for keeping secrets! He gave me those flares before we started.
And I—I never told you!" Greta seemed ready for
tears.

"It might be a great deal worse," Percy O'Hara
broke in. His tone was reassuring. He seated himself
comfortably on a mossy rock. "I think that scream
really meant trouble of some sort. It would seem
to be our duty to investigate. And when there's in-
vestigating to be done there's safety in numbers. I
think we'll do well to await the arrival of your
friend. Perhaps someone will come with him.

"By the way," his tone changed and his bright
eyes gleamed in the firelight, "have I been smelling
bacon, coffee, and all that these days, or have I not?"

"Pure imagination!" Jane laughed. "We live on
nuts and berries." For all her laughing denial, she set
about the task of sending delicious aromas drifting
along the slope of Greenstone Ridge.

The "phantom's" delight in the food set before
him could not have been denied. No empty words

Jane Set About Preparing a Lunch

of praise were his. For all that, fingers that trembled ever so slightly, eyes that smiled in a way one could not forget, told Jane her skill as a brewer of coffee and a broiler of bacon was appreciated fully.

When the simple meal had ended, with a low fire of bright coals gleaming red on the great flat rock, they settled themselves upon cushions of moss to wait.

"Wait for what?" Greta asked herself. "For the coming of Vincent Stearns. And then?"

Who could find an answer? Before her mind's eye the seaplane once more soared aloft to at last settle down upon that narrow lake. She looked again upon those black waters, saw the rowboat, the moving figures, the helpless one being carried away.

"What does it mean?" she whispered. Then again she seemed to hear that piercing scream.

All this occupied her alert mind only a few short moments. Then her dark inquiring eyes were upon the face of that man who sat staring dreamily at the fire.

"Percy O'Hara!" she whispered low. "And the phantom violin! Why is he here?"

As if feeling her eyes upon him, he turned half about, favored her with a matchless smile, opened his lips as if to speak, then seeming to think better of it, turned his face once more toward the fire.

"Oh!" she thought, "he was going to tell me

something!"

But he did not speak. Instead he continued to stare at the fire. She studied his face. That face was well worth her study. It was a rather handsome, strong, sensitive face, an honest, kindly face. She looked in vain for traces of deep sorrow. They were not to be found. She tried casting him in the role of a man fleeing from justice. It could not be done.

"And yet why is he here?" she thought.

Once again his eyes were upon her.

This time he took his violin from its case by his side. Tucking it under his chin, he began to play. The music did not seem to be made by man. So fine, so all but silent was it, yet so exquisitely beautiful, it might have been the song of a bird on the wing, or angels in heaven.

"Oh!" Greta breathed as the last faint note died away, and again "Oh!"

Wrapping the priceless instrument carefully, he returned it to its case.

"Now," she whispered, "now the phantom will tell his story." Still he did not speak.

"Perhaps," she told herself, "he is wondering what lies in the future for him, the immediate future, when he goes down the hill to that—that place down there."

She looked at his fingers. Slim, delicate, they were the fingers of an artist. "And with these he will de-

fend someone," she told herself as a little thrill crept
up her back. "How—how impossible that seems!

"And yet, great musicians are not cowards." She
was thinking of that celebrated Polish patriot who,
having played for the rich and great of all lands, had
put aside his music when his country called and
served it faithfully.

"He will not tell us tonight," she assured herself.
"The phantom will not speak, perhaps never at all.
Secrets are our own. No one has a right to pry into
our lives."

Only once during that long wait did the phantom
speak. Turning to Greta, he said, "Where are you
staying on the island?"

Greta nodded at the small tent. "Right here," she
said.

"But before that?"

"We have been living on the wreck of the 'Pilgrim'."

"The wreck!" His eyes shone. "How wonderful!
Better than Greenstone Ridge. Only," he added,
"people would come to see you there."

"Yes. And you will come?" Greta's tone was eager
with anticipation.

Once again his eyes shone upon her. "Yes," he
said quietly, "I fancy I shall be doing just that sometime."

It was a promise in answer to a prayer. The girl

could ask no more.

Ten minutes later there came the sound of movement in the bushes some distance down the ridge. This was followed by a loud, "Yoo hoo!"

CHAPTER TWENTY-THREE

MUSICAL ENCHANTMENT

"Yoo hoo! What's up?" came from below.

"It's Vincent Stearns!" Greta sprang to her feet. She cast one wistful glance toward Percy O'Hara. He, too, was on the move.

"The spell is broken," she told herself with a sigh. "His story will not be told, at least, not now. Perhaps never."

"Nothing of importance has happened," Greta said aloud to Vincent Stearns as he came toiling up the slope. "At least not to us. It was just an accident. Jane fell over a flare and kicked it into the fire. We—"

"A fortunate accident I should say!" Percy O'Hara's tone was full of meaning. "As far as we can tell, there's something going on down there by that little lake that needs looking into. And now we have reinforcements."

"This sounds like an adventure." The young newspaper photographer's face took on a look of unwonted animation. "I'll turn reporter and get a scoop for my paper."

"When we have finished you may not be in a mood for writing." Percy O'Hara did not smile as he said this.

In as few words as possible he told the little they knew of the mysterious ones who came and went in an airplane and who uttered unearthly screams in the night. "We might as well get right down there and have the thing over with at once," he added at the end. "I don't like interfering any more than I like being interfered with. It has been more than a year since I went into voluntary exile up here." He paused to look away at the forest and distant waters all aglimmer with the light of the moon.

"Voluntary exile," Greta thought, "I wonder why? Can it have been anything very terrible that drove him into seclusion? He does not appear to fear being taken back."

"I've been thankful for the solitude," Percy went on. "But there are times when one has no right to be left alone. Those people down there appear to have forfeited that right.

"I have a light rifle," he added. "I thought I might use it sometimes to kill rabbits if necessity demanded it. I've never used it."

"I've a gun of a sort," Vincent added his bit. "I have a notion that persuasion is better than firearms, though. What say we get going? Young ladies—"

"We're coming along," Jane put in. "I'll do my part if need be, and Greta can be the nurse, in—in case—" She did not finish.

"But you're lame!" Percy protested.

"Only a little. Some raven came along with bandages and liniment." She smiled knowingly. "It's just about got me fixed up."

They were away. It was strange, this little rescue party trooping away down the ridge, single file, in the night.

"W-weird!" Greta whispered to her companion. "What do you think it is?"

"Pr—probably nothing." Jane was all aquiver.

Working their way silently down the hillside, they at last came to the lower plateau. Here they came upon a well-worn moose trail that, they thought, must lead to the lake.

They were not mistaken. Before they reached the shore they caught the sound of splashing.

"Moose." Greta's lips formed the word she did not speak.

Looking across the lake, they caught a dull glow of light.

"That—that's the place." She could not prevent her teeth from chattering.

"We'll have to follow round the shore of the lake." Percy O'Hara marched on as once more they took up the trail leading to the mysterious cottage.

For a full half hour they moved silently through the evergreen forest that skirted the lake. The low plump-plump of feet on a mossy trail, the swish of

They Worked Their Way Down the Hillside

branches, were all that broke the silence.

At last, quite suddenly, they came to a narrow cleared space, and there at its back was the house of mystery.

For a moment they stood there, the four of them, Greta, Jane, Percy O'Hara, and Vincent Stearns, before a low structure that, standing dark and threatening among the black spruce trees and shadows of night, seemed to dare them to move forward. With her own eyes Greta had seen a helpless person carried from an airplane to this place. Three times with her own ears she had heard an unearthly scream rise from this spot. And now, now as the hour approached midnight they stood there listening, breathing hard, waiting. Waiting for what?

Not a sound, save the low splash of a moose feeding from the bottom of the lake, reached their ears. From the single window, small and low, a dull light gleamed. The place seemed asleep.

And yet, the instant Vincent tapped lightly on the door a hand was on the latch. "Now—" Greta took a step forward. "Now—"

The door was thrown open. A man, seeming very tall and thin in that dull light, stood before them. His voice when he spoke was low, melodious, friendly, and quite disarming. There was, too, a note of sadness.

"Come in! Have you lost your way? May I help

you?" he said.

Greta at this moment recalled those startling screams, and shuddered.

There was about the place an air of comfort. A gasp of surprise escaped Greta's lips. "Chairs, couches, books, fireplace. This might be the living-room of any home. And up here!"

"We—we've made a mistake," she whispered to Jane. This was indeed a strange hide-out for a kid-naper, and the man who opened the door did not look like a kidnaper.

"Wait!" was the answer.

The silence grew painful. "No," Percy O'Hara said at last, as if there had been no silence. "We didn't lose our way. In fact I could not lose myself up here if I tried. I've lived on this ridge for more than a year. We came—"

"Wait!" The tall man, whose hair was graying about the temples, held up a hand. "You need not go on. I understand perfectly. I—I'm sorry you came. But since you are here, you have a right to be told certain things. Won't you be seated?"

He drew chairs to the fire, chairs with deep, soft cushions. As she sank into one of these Greta thought with a shudder how difficult it would be to rise from such a chair in a hurry, should necessity demand it.

"I—" their host began, "I am considered a rich man. In fact a company I control owns more than

half this island. This shelter rests on my land. You
have been camping, all of you, on my land." He
paused as if to permit the words to sink in.

"It is supposed," he went on at last, "that rich
men are the privileged ones of earth. The truth is
they have few privileges. Here I am at the heart of
an all but deserted island, living on my own land. I
own every foot of land within ten miles of this spot!
And yet, when I choose, I cannot be alone!"

"I wish we hadn't come!" Greta whispered.

"Wait!" Jane replied once more.

At this juncture a very short, chubby man with an
air of briskness about him entered the room.

"Ah!" He rubbed his small hands together. "We
have company, Percy O'Hara, Vincent Stearns,
Greta Bronson, and Jane Withers."

Greta started. How could this little man know
their names? She was to wonder still more.

"You have no notion, Mr. Van Zandt," the little
man said, turning to his tall companion, "how famous our company is! A successful newspaper photographer, a very famous violinist, not to speak of
the lady violinist and a well-known actress."

He turned to the astonished group. "Your arrival
has saved me the bother of hunting you up—provid-
ing now I may count upon your services."

Never had the two girls found themselves in so
strange a position. They had come here with the

others to assist—assist in what?

Vincent half rose, then dropped back to his place. Percy O'Hara gripped the arms of his chair. Only Jane appeared at ease, and it was she who at last spoke. "I am sure," she replied evenly, "that we shall be glad to render any service possible to Doctor Prince."

Once again Greta stared, this time at Jane. How could Jane know this man?

"Ah!" the little man replied, not denying his identity, "I had hoped so. It is, however, from your musical friends that I expect to secure aid.

"Mr. Van Zandt," he addressed the other respectfully, "have I your permission to inform them?"

A pained expression passed over the man's face as he nodded assent.

The next day, just as the shadows were beginning to lengthen on the hillside, Greta found herself joined in an undertaking the like of which she had never before known. Her part seemed as simple as the song of a bird who on a branch far above her head warbled in his own sweet way; yet she threw into it every atom of her being.

Seated on a moss-covered rock a stone's throw from the mysterious lodge, she tucked her violin under her chin and played as she had never done before. The tunes that crept out from that evergreen forest, like songs from the heart, were old as life itself, yet known and loved by every generation. She played one of those sweet, melodious songs of twilight, written as only an inspired artist can compose, then rested with bow poised, waiting. From away on the hill across the narrow lake the notes came back to her.

Not an echo, but the crystal clear notes of a second violin, played as only one musician could play them, Percy O'Hara.

Once again she played the slow, dreamy refrain. And, as before, it came drifting back to her.

Inside the lodge Jane, listening, caught the rise and fall of the song.

But strange events were passing. Before her in a great cushioned chair sat a boy of fourteen. His attractive face was as white as death.

"Think!" The little doctor, looking into the boy's face, spoke softly. "Think, think back, back, back. What frightens you? Why do you cry out? Think back."

He leaned forward. Through the open window floated the entrancing music. Jane, understanding the meaning and the terrible import of it all, scarcely breathed, yet her lips moved in prayer.

"Think!" the doctor repeated. "Think back. Now you are twelve, skating, playing football, wandering through the forest. Do you see anything that terrifies you?"

No answer.

"Now you are ten." The doctor's words came in a whisper. "You are on roller skates. You are at home by the fire. You speed in an automobile. Are you terribly afraid?"

Still no answer. Still the music, now faint, now strong, came floating through the open window.

"Now you are six." The doctor's eyes shone. "You are by the fireside. You are in your own small room. It is night. Does—"

Of a sudden there came a scream so piercing that Jane leaped to her feet. It was the boy. His face was distorted by an agony of fear.

"What? What is it?" The doctor was bending over the boy. "What frightens you?"

"The dog!" the boy cried. "The big shaggy dog! Don't let him in! He will bite me!"

"No! No! You are mistaken. That is a kind dog. He will not bite you. He has never harmed any one. You must learn to love the good old shaggy fellow."

The lines of distortion began to disappear from the boy's face. There was a question and a gleam of hope in his eyes.

Through the window, borne on the breeze, there floated the notes of a song,

"Silent night, silent night,
Lovely and bright—"

"He is kind," the boy murmured. "He will not

bite." The look on his face was growing peaceful. He leaned back in his chair and was soon lost in quiet slumber.

"You see," the doctor murmured low as they tiptoed from the room, "God, with our help, is working a cure. Tomorrow we will repeat this. By that time the demon of fear will have left him."

"And it was his scream we heard," Jane said softly.

"It was his scream," the father of the boy, the rich Mr. Van Zandt, replied. "It is a form of hysteria brought on by fright. He has suffered long, and we have suffered with him. We hoped this secluded spot might help. It did no good. When the illusion came he was seized with terror. He screamed. But now, thanks to this good doctor and the mystery of music, we may hope for a complete cure."

"These cases," the doctor said, assuming a professional air, "are strange, but not uncommon. At some time in the patient's past he has been terribly frightened. His outer self may have forgotten; his deep, inner self has not. When conditions arise that suggest this fright, it recurs.

"If we can still his mind, then cause him to think back, back, back to that time of great fright, we may be able to reassure his inner self, and the hysteria will vanish.

"We hope to banish this terrifying dog, who in reality could not have been vicious at all, then our work will be done."

"That," said Greta some time later as she sat in the boat near the lodge, "is one of the strangest things I have ever known."

"Our minds *are* strange," said Jane as she rowed slowly toward the shore nearest their home on the ridge. "But that," she murmured after a time, "that which we witnessed today is no less than musical enchantment."

CHAPTER TWENTY-FOUR

THE LITTLE BLACK TRAMP

It was evening of the following day. The fire on that big flat rock burned brightly. Jane and Greta sat sipping hot chocolate. For a full half hour, while twilight faded into night, neither spoke.

It was Greta who broke the silence. "Jane," she said soberly, "life is strange."

"Yes," Jane agreed.

"Here we are on Greenstone Ridge," the dark-eyed girl went on. "We came here to explore and to—to search out the secrets of the phantom. We found the phantom. We solved the mystery. And yet—"

"The phantom is more mysterious than before." Jane smiled a dreamy smile.

"Yes," Greta replied quickly, "he is! And perhaps we shall never solve this mystery. We have not seen him since that night when we marched down upon that mysterious cabin by the lake—the day we helped the little boy."

"We have heard his music but have not seen him, your strange Percy O'Hara," Jane said quietly. "I wonder why he is alone so much of the time."

This was exactly true. When the strange little doc-

tor had suggested that they assist him in his marvelous cure of that boy afflicted with mental terror,
Percy O'Hara had agreed at once, but had suggested that Greta should furnish the music close at
hand and that his should be little more than an echo.
This arranged, he had slipped away into the night.
Since then they had heard him twice, had seen him
not at all.

"Why?" Greta whispered to herself. "Why?"
There came no answer.

"Jane," she said, springing to her feet, "our work
here is done. Doctor Prince has told us that our as-
sistance is no longer needed. As for the phan—phantom, Percy O'Hara, we have no right to pry into his
affairs. I—I'd like to go down to the camping ground
by Duncan's Bay."

"Tonight?" Jane rose slowly to her feet. She, too,
felt ready to leave the Ridge.

"Tonight."

"All right." Jane began stuffing things into her
bag. "We'll be on our way in a jiffy. As soon as we
get things packed."

A half hour later two dark figures, guided only by
a flashlight, made their way over the long moose trail
leading along the ridge, thence down to the shores
of a dark and silent bay. And all the time Greta was
thinking of Percy O'Hara, who had charmed thousands upon thousands with his matchless music, hid-

ing away there on the ridge. Once she whispered, "Green eyes, a hundred pairs of green eyes. How very strange!"

As they neared the shores of the bay, however, her thoughts returned to her friend Jeanne and their home, the wreck of the old *Pilgrim*. Once she whispered low, "A barrel of gold."

Had you chanced to look down upon that narrow stretch of level land on the shores of Duncan's Bay later that night, you might have spied, hidden away in a shadowy corner, a small tent. Beneath that tent two girls slept, Jane and Greta. For them Greenstone Ridge had become a memory.

They were up at dawn. Their boat, hidden deep among some scrub spruce trees, awaited them. So did a bright and shimmering lake. And beyond this, dark and silent, was their home, the wreck. It seemed a long time since they had been there.

"Perhaps Jeanne has come back," said Jane. "We will row over to the wreck at once and see if we can find her."

They had covered half the distance to the wreck and were watching eagerly for some sign of life on its sloping decks, when Greta, whose gaze had strayed away to the left, cried out quite suddenly, "Look, Jane! What is that over there?"

Shading her eyes, Jane followed the younger girl's gaze, then said with a slow tone of assurance, "It's a boat, a small black boat adrift. Some ship, or perhaps a schooner, has lost her lifeboat. We'll take it in tow, and tie it up over at the wreck. Whoever has lost it can get it there."

The small black boat was soon tied behind their own, and Jane rowed again toward their home, the wreck.

Greta had climbed on board the wreck, Jane had finished tying up her own boat and was giving her attention to the small black tramp, when she noted something of mild interest. In the bottom of that boat was water two or three inches deep, from a rain, perhaps. Floating on the surface of that water was a small square of paper.

"That might give some clue," she thought as she put out a hand.

Once she had spread the paper on the boat's seat, her lips parted in surprise.

"Greta!" she cried, "Greta! Come here. See what I have found!"

When Greta arrived all she saw was a sheet of water-soaked paper. In the center of that paper, written with a purple pencil, badly blurred but still quite easily read, were four words:

"A BARREL OF GOLD."

"Isn't that strange!" Jane exclaimed. "Here we've been dreaming in a silly sort of way about a barrel of gold. And now, here it is, all written out by a stranger!"

"Perhaps Jeanne wrote it," Greta suggested thoughtfully.

"She can't have. It's not her writing. And look!" Jane studied the paper more closely. "There are two lines drawn under those words as if some other words had been crossed out and these inserted. And that—" she straightened up, "that is exactly what happened. There are faint traces of pencil marks all over the paper. The water has about washed them away. Perhaps when the paper is dry we can read the entire message."

Placing the paper carefully on her outspread hand, she carried it to the deck, then smoothed it out on a board in the sun.

"Jeanne is not here," Greta said quietly. "She's not been here. Everything is just as we left it, except—" she hesitated.

"Except what?" Jane stared.

"I can't be sure, but I think there are fresh marks of a black schooner that has been tied up alongside this wreck. Come and see."

"There can't be any doubt of it," Jane agreed a few moments later. "The black schooner has been here again, Greta! Greta!" She gripped the slender girl's arm. "Do you suppose there could have been a barrel of gold hidden on this wreck? And have they carried it away?

"Of course not!" she exploded, answering her own question. "There are three or four barrels of oil in the hold. That was all they left. Swen told us that, and he should know."

CHAPTER TWENTY-FIVE

FATHER SUPERIOR TAKES A HAND

The paper taken from the *Little Black Tramp,* as Jane had named the derelict, proved a disappointment. Though there was still some suggestion of writing remaining on its surface after it was dry, not one word could be read. Only those four words, brighter than ever, stood out clear and strong, "A BARREL OF GOLD."

Without the sprightly Jeanne about, the wreck seemed a lonely place. "What do you say we row back to the camping ground and dig for treasure?" Jane suggested after their midday siesta. "We can stay all night if the wind blows up."

"Dig for treasure? Jane, you're still thinking of that barrel of gold!" Greta exclaimed. "You'll not find it there. It's hidden on this old ship. You wait and see!"

Greta was glad enough to go. She hoped, for one thing, that she might catch again the tuneful notes of that phantom violin. "Shall I ever know," she asked herself, "why Percy O'Hara hides away on Greenstone Ridge?" She closed her eyes to see again that bushy mass of gray hair, those frank, smiling young eyes. "Percy O'Hara. How much good he could be doing! How he can charm the world's cares away! And how this poor old world needs to have its cares charmed away!

"And he could help those who are struggling up. He could teach—" She dared not continue, dared not hope that sometime, somewhere, this matchless musician might take her bow gently from her hand as he said with that marvelous smile, "No, my child. Not that way. See! Listen!" And then he would play for her.

"If only it might be!" she sighed. Yes, she wanted to go ashore, longed to climb all the way up Greenstone Ridge. But this last she was resolved never to do. "He said he would come," she whispered, "and he will."

That night Greta slept soundly beneath the tent on the camping grounds. Having listened in vain for the faintest tremor of music on the air, she had at last fallen asleep.

Jane, too, was beneath the blankets, but she did not sleep. The strange discovery of that day was still on her mind. "Barrel of gold," she repeated more than once.

Her treasure hunt that afternoon had been singularly unsuccessful. She had not found so much as a flint arrowhead or a copper penny.

"It's a big piece of nonsense!" she told herself. "And yet it's fun."

A half hour later, having dragged on shoes, **slacks,** and sweater, she was digging once more on **the** camping ground, digging for gold.

She had stirred up their campfire and was digging with the aid of its light. As she labored her sturdy figure cast odd, fantastic shadows on the dark forest at her back.

At the same hour Jeanne returned to the wreck. She came with her gypsy friends on the *Ship of Joy.* For once in his life Bihari was in a great rush. His journey round the island had been completed. There was in the air some deep prophecy of storm. Being one of those who live their lives out of doors, he felt rather than saw this.

"They are here!" Jeanne cried in great joy as they neared the wreck of the old *Pilgrim.* "Jane and Greta must be here!"

"But there is no light," someone on the boat protested.

"They are dreaming in some corner of the ship, or perhaps they are asleep," Jeanne insisted. "They *must* be here, for—see! There is their boat. We have but one boat. They could not well be away from the ship when their boat is here."

Climbing to the deck, the little French girl bade her gypsy friends a fond farewell, then from her favorite spot on the deck watched the lights of Bihari's boat grow dim in the distance. Then she set about

Jane Had Gone Ashore

the task of finding her friends. This was to be a hard task. They were not there.

The explanation is simple enough. Having tried out the *Little Black Tramp* and found it easy to row, Jane had chosen to go ashore in it and to leave her own boat tied up to the wreck. So here it was and here was the little French girl alone on the *Pilgrim*. It was night, and she had not forgotten Bihari's warning: "There comes a great storm."

On the camping ground, lighted by the campfire's flickering glow, Jane dug steadily on. "Not that I expect to find anything," she told herself. "I'm just wearing down my mental resistance to sleep. Pretty soon I'll drop this old spade and creep beneath the blankets. I'll—"

She broke off short. Strange sounds reached her ears; at least they were strange for this place. Music, the tones of a violin, came to her. Clear and distinct they were.

"It can't be far," she told herself. She thought of Percy O'Hara, the phantom.

"The air's strange tonight," she told herself. "Perhaps he's still away up there. Sound carries a long way at times."

Once again her spade cut deep in the sand. But now her heart skipped a beat. She had struck some solid object.

"It's probably only a rock or a log buried by a

storm," she told herself. "And yet—" She was dig-
ing fiercely now. Like a dog close to a ground squir-
rel's nest, she made the dirt fly.

The thing she had found was not a rock. "It's not
hard enough for that," she told herself. "A log?
Well, perhaps. But it—it's—"

She ceased digging. Seizing a firebrand, she
fanned it into flame, then held it low in the hole she
had dug. The next instant she was all but bowled
over with astonishment.

"It *is* a barrel!" she breathed. "Or, at least, a keg.
And it has heavy copper hoops. It—"

But at this instant a light shone full upon her
face. It was there for only an instant, but it was long
enough to give her warning. Seizing her spade, she
had half filled the hole when a small boat came
around the point.

At that hour too there were strange doings on the
wreck. The mysterious black schooner had returned.
Only chance had prevented the men on the schooner
from seeing the light that shone from Jeanne's
cabin. They approached the wreck from the other
side.

The first suggestion of their presence came to
Jeanne as a slight bump ran through the stout old
hull.

"A—a boat!" she breathed. Instantly her light was
out. A moment had not elapsed before, wrapped in

a long dark coat and with a dark scarf thrown over her head, she crept out on the deck.

Once outside, she stood there, silent, intent, ready to flee, listening.

"Chains," she whispered at last, "I hear them. That's what they had on that black schooner that other night. They mean to lift something with chains. I'll creep along the deck to that box where life preservers were kept. I'll have a look at these men from there. They won't see me. I'll be in the shadows."

She crept along the deck keeping hidden in the deep shadows.

"Here—here's the place." She drew up behind a large box painted white.

After a brief rest to quiet the wild beating of her heart, she crept forward.

"There!" she whispered. "I can see them plainly from here. There's the man in the diving rig again. He is just going over the side. He's taking a chain with him. I can hear it rattle. The chain's fast to a light cable. They're going to try lifting something from below, that's certain."

The diver disappeared beneath black waters. Two other men stood at attention. The girl held her breath and waited. She tried to picture to herself the inside of the ship beneath the water.

"There are the cabins where people have slept.

Fish are swimming there and big old crawfish crawl-
ing over the berths. The deck is slippery with slime,
and the hold where all the freight was stored is dark
as a dungeon. You'd think—"

She did not finish. From the distance had come a
strange sound. A rushing as of a mighty wind. "But
there's no wind!"

The sound increased in volume until it was like
the roar of a storm. Then, suddenly, a great swell
struck the ship. It set the old wreck shuddering from
stem to stern. It picked up the black schooner and,
tossing it high, landed it half upon the dry deck of
the ship and half upon the water. It keeled over on
one side, reeled like a drunken man, seemed about
to turn square over, then sliding off the deck, went
gliding away.

"But the diver?" Once again the girl held her
breath.

After what seemed a very long time, a dark spot
appeared off to the right. The power boat glided
over. The dark spot was taken on board.

The next moment a second swell shook the ship.
When this wave had subsided the power boat was
nowhere to be seen.

"Good old Father Superior," the little French girl
exclaimed. "He took a hand!

"Will they return?" she asked herself. She found
no answer. A glance away to the left caused her to

shudder. Like an army of black demons, clouds were massed low against the sky. A faint flash of light painted them a lurid hue. This was repeated three times. Then all was darker than before.

CHAPTER TWENTY-SIX

THE PASSING OF THE 'PILGRIM'

Jane had scarcely concealed the newly-discovered treasure before she knew, from the shape of the oncoming boat, that it was owned by a friend. In truth it was Swen with his stout little fishing boat.

"Hello!" he shouted as the fire, flaring up, revealed her face. "I thought you were at home on the wreck. I saw a light there. I was sure of it. Had to come in there for some nets I left on the shore, then I was going over to see how you were getting on and to warn you."

"No," said Jane, "there can't be a light on the wreck. No one is there."

"Yes," Swen's tone carried conviction. "There *was* a light."

"Then," said Jane, "Jeanne has returned, or— or someone else is there.

"Greta!" she called. "Greta! Wake up! Someone is on the wreck. We must go there.

"We'll leave the tent as it is," she said five minutes later as Greta, hastily dressed and half asleep, stepped out in the air of night.

"I'll take you over," Swen said. "The sea is roughing up a bit."

"Swen," Jane said as they went pop-popping through the Narrows, "you said you meant to warn us. Warn us of what?"

"Probably nothing." Swen seemed ill at ease. "There'll be a storm—just a storm, that's all. Two waves, like tidal waves, came near swamping my boat. It's a sign, the fishermen say. But then, we are superstitious. That's it, I guess."

For all that, when he had landed the girls at the wreck and had made sure Jeanne, not some stranger, was there, he turned his boat about and steamed away at full speed.

"He came to warn us," Jane whispered to herself. Then a matter of overwhelming interest drove all other thoughts from her mind. She turned to the others.

"Oh, girls!" she exclaimed. "Just think! I found a barrel, a small barrel!"

"On the camping ground?" Jeanne leaped to her feet.

"Nowhere else."

"And—and what was in it?" Greta was fairly dancing with excitement.

"There wasn't time to see. It had copper hoops, that's all I know. Swen came and then—then we went away. I—I covered it up. It won't run away," she laughed as Jeanne's face sobered. "It will keep for another day."

"But let us go now, tonight!" Jeanne was quite beside herself with excitement.

"No, not tonight," Jane said with an air of decision. "Tomorrow."

As things turned out it was to be that night, but this she could not know.

Some three hours later Jane stirred uneasily in her sleep. It was a very dark night. The cabin on the wrecked *Pilgrim* in which she slept was a well of darkness. Yet there were times when, for one brief second, every detail of the cabin showed out in bold relief. The over-ornamented walls, done in white and gold, the narrow shelf where a small clock ticked loudly, the rough table with two short legs and two long ones to make up for the slanting deck; all these could be seen plainly. So too could the blonde hair of her bunk-mate, Jeanne, sleeping beside her in the berth where for forty years only ship captains had slept.

Jane stirred again. One brown arm stole from beneath the covers. The hand seemed to reach for some object hung in space.

"A barrel of gold." Her lips said the words aloud. The sound of her own voice roused her to a state of half-awakeness. "A barrel of gold," she repeated.

For some little time she lay there half asleep, half awake.

Her sleep had been disturbed by certain sounds,

distant rumbles, rushes and swishes of water; also by those vivid flashes of light.

A moment more and she sat bolt upright in bed.

"It's going to storm," she mumbled to herself, without being greatly disturbed. It had stormed before. Three times great, dark clouds had come driving in across black waters to engulf them. Each time the wrecked *Pilgrim*, with her three last passengers on board, had weathered the storm in as stalwart a manner as any ship afloat on the sea.

For some time she sat there listening, watching. As the flashes of light grew brighter, more frequent, and the rumbles broke into short, sharp crashes, she crept silently from beneath the covers to draw on a heavy jacket and then stepped out upon the deck.

At once a cold chill seized her. A flash of lightning had revealed such a cloud as she had not seen in all her life. Inky black, straight up and down like a gigantic pillar, it appeared to glide across waters that reflected its ink-blackness and to grow—grow—grow as it advanced.

Stepping quickly back into the cabin, she shook her companions into wakefulness.

"Jeanne! Greta! Wake up! It is going to storm. Something rather terrible!"

Instantly she went about the business of lighting a candle. Then she drew on slacks and shoes.

Her mind was in a whirl, yet she managed to

maintain a certain degree of inner calm.

What was to be done? Here they were, three girls on board a wreck with a storm that promised to be violent, sweeping down upon them.

There was but one way of leaving the wreck. They must go, if at all, in their sixteen-foot rowboat—a mere nutshell in such a storm as this promised to become.

"Are—are you dressed?" Jane called to the girls in a shaky voice.

"Yes, all dressed." Both Jeanne and Greta appeared to be quite calm.

"All right. Throw what things you can into your suitcases, then come on." She set the example by tossing garments into a corner, then cramming them into her bag.

Having thrust a flashlight into her pocket, she led the way out into the night.

She was met by a gust of wind that all but blew her off the deck.

"Look—look out!" she warned. "Hang on tight! Over here! The boat's over here."

To leave the ship at such a time as this seemed madness. Yet there had come to her a sense of guidance. In times of great crisis she had more than once experienced just this. Now she moved like one directed by a master hand.

The water appeared blacker now. The flashes of

light were vivid beyond belief. The swells were coming in. Great sweeping swells, they lifted the little
rowboat, tied on the lee side of the wreck, to a pro-
digious height, then dropped it into a well of darkness.

"Drop—drop your bag into the boat when it comes
—comes up." Wind seemed to fill Jane's ears. It
caught her words and cast them away.

Down went the bags, and with them the boat into
the trough of a big wave.

One, two, three, up surged the boat again on the
crest of a wave.

"Now! Over you go!" Seizing Greta, she fairly
threw her into the boat.

Her heart sank with the boat. It rose with it as
well. Jeanne was next. A moment more and she was
over the side, clinging to the seat, cutting the rope,
seizing the oars, then shoving off, all in one wild
breath.

"We—we'll keep—keep our stern to the storm!"
she screamed. "Head in toward Duncan's Bay. Some
sandy beaches there. Mi—might land. Mi—" The
wind blew the words from her throat.

The cove that forms an approach to Duncan's
Bay is shaped like the top of an hourglass. At the
seaward side it is a mile wide. At the land side it is
tapered to a narrow channel. By great good fortune
the wind was shoreward and slightly toward the en-

*"We'll Head in Toward Duncan's Bay," Jane
Shouted*

trance of Duncan's Bay. Jane's hope was to work her boat back into this cove where, more and more protected by the reef, she might find calmer water and less wind.

To ride a great storm in a rowboat is always thrilling, but not certainly too dangerous. If the waves are long and high, you may ride to their crest, glide down the other side, then rise again.

Pulling with all her might, the young oarsman held her boat's stern to the gale. They rose. They fell. They rose again, this time in the midst of hissing foam.

"This—this is going to be worth telling," she shrieked. "If we live to tell it."

Now and again sharp flashes of lightning revealed their position. They were working back into the cove. But each moment the storm grew wilder. The wind fairly shrieked in their ears. Their hair flew out wildly. Some sea bird, seeking shelter, shot past them at a wild speed.

Clinging to one another, Jeanne and Greta sat in the stern. As Greta watched that onrushing pillar of cloud, she was all but overcome by the conviction that never again would they romp upon the deck of the ill-fated ship.

"And we have known such joy there!" she told herself with a low sob. "Our swimming pool, long, lazy hours in the sun, songs at sunset."

Then a strange question crept into her mind. What was it the men on the black schooner had sought on the wreck? What had they expected to find in the hold of the old ship?

"Whatever it was," she said to herself, "they will never find it now. This storm will break up the 'Pilgrim' and whatever these men sought will go to the bottom of the lake. Only Father Superior will know the secret."

Then the storm broke. A vivid flash revealed the dark column of cloud. It appeared to hover over the *Pilgrim*.

"Oh!" Greta covered here eyes.

Jane still stared straight away and continued to row. This was no time for flinching. She saw the battered wreck rise high in air. After that came moments of intense darkness, such darkness as seems solid, like a black wall at the dead of night.

When at last the blackness lifted, a flash of light showed the pillar of cloud far away and on the reef there was not a sign of the ill-fated ship, the *Pilgrim*. The old ship had had its last passenger.

"Look!" Jeanne cried, pointing away in the other direction. "Look over there! A light!"

There could be no mistaking it. Off toward the entrance to Duncan's Harbor was a swaying, blinking light.

It's a boat. Some sort of a boat. We—we'll try to

head that way.

"The ship," Jane said soberly a moment later, "is gone! It was like an arm, that cloud, a great black arm reaching down and picking it up. I saw it. A waterspout, I suppose they'd call it. We—we were saved by God's guidance."

A short time later they found themselves approaching a small power boat that, tossing about over the waves, moved cautiously nearer their own boat.

To their great joy they found this to be Swen, and with him was Vincent Stearns.

"I didn't want to leave you," Swen said a trifle shamefacedly, once he had them on board and well within the Narrows. "I was afraid. But when I saw that cloud, when I knew what was sure to happen, I got Vincent to come with me. Now here we are, and, thank God, you are safe!"

"Listen!" It was Greta who held up a hand for silence as they passed out of the Narrows. Music had reached her ears, wild, delirious music, such as one may produce only at the end of a terrific storm.

The storm was over—there could be no questioning that. The moon was out in all its glory. And there, his gray hair glistening in that light, standing before their tent on the camping ground, was the phantom, Percy O'Hara. He was playing as perhaps he had never played before.

"Now," Greta whispered, "I have found him. I shall never lose him again."

Jane, you might say, was strange. At this dramatic moment she was thinking to herself, "A barrel, a copper-bound barrel. A barrel of gold."

CHAPTER TWENTY-SEVEN

THE GREEN-EYED MANSION

"A barrel of gold!" Jane cried as the music ceased and she sprang ashore. "Come on! A copper-bound barrel! A barrel of gold!" She was able to keep her secret no longer.

Forgetting all else, Jeanne, Swen, and Vincent followed her. Not so Greta. She had found her mysterious friend once more. She would throw discretion and all conventions to the wind.

"You—you will tell me?" She hurried up to the musician smiling there in the moonlight.

"Why, yes, my sweet little girl, if it will bring you joy I will tell you my secret which, after all—" he motioned her to a seat on a log by the fire, "is truly no secret at all.

"Being famous," he said, smiling in a strange way, "is not all that men think it. To hear people say, 'Here he comes! There he goes!' and to know they mean you, to be stared at all day long! Who could wish for that?"

"But you charmed them with your music," Greta said in a low tone.

"Yes," he agreed, "that was not so bad. To stand before thousands, to know that you are truly bringing joy to their lives, that is grand.

"But even that—" his voice took on a weary note, "even that loses its charm when you are weary and they still say, 'Play for us. Play here. Play there.' Then you long to be away from it all, to forget, and to make a fresh start.

"And so," he added, smiling down at her, "so I ran away to Greenstone Ridge.

"One more thing—" his tone became more deeply serious. "I wanted to create a little music of my own, all my own. I suppose the desire to create is in the heart of all. Up there alone on Greenstone Ridge I wrote music. I played it to the birds, the wolves, the moose, but mainly to the twittering birds. You have heard some of it. How—how do you like it?"

"I think," Greta whispered, "that it is divine!

"But now—" Greta's tone was wistful. "Now you will come back and you will play again! And you will teach others?"

"Yes." There was a touch of tenderness in his voice. "Yes, dear little girl, I will go back now. I will teach others, and you shall be my very first pupil."

"Oh!" she breathed. "How—how marvelous! But—" her voice sank to a whisper. "We—we are not rich."

"Rich? Who spoke of money?" Once more he beamed down upon her. "No true artist wants money from his disciples. All he asks is that his pupils have the touch divine. And that, my child, is yours. It is your very great gift."

For a time there was silence beside the campfire. That silence was broken by a shout of laughter. It came from the party of treasure hunters. Jane's barrel had been dragged from its sandy hiding place.

"I'll just break in the head with the spade," she said as it lay on its side.

"No! No!" Vincent Stearns took the spade from her. Setting the barrel on end, he rubbed the sand away to find a wooden cork. With the heavy handle of his hunting knife he drove this in, and at once a pungent odor filled the air.

"Rum!" said Vincent. "Very old rum!"

"And not gold?" Jane's hopes fell.

"Just rum," the photographer repeated. "Some trader buried it years ago. Poor fellow! He never came back!"

"I—I'll pour it out." Jane's hand was on the small barrel.

"Oh, I—I wouldn't do that!" Once again Vincent intervened. "They say old rum is very good for colds. That right, Swen?"

"Sure it is, in the winter." Swen smiled broadly.

"Leave it to Swen and me," Vincent suggested. And so it was left.

"But those green eyes I saw up on the ridge," Greta was saying to Percy O'Hara. "I saw them twice. They were horrible."

"That," Percy O'Hara chuckled, "was the light from my green-eyed mansion.

"You see," he laughed again, "I found a great many greenstones on the ridge. One day I got a grinding wheel from Swen's little store."

"He told me," she murmured.

"I left money for it. I polished the stones and set them in some soft sort of rock for tiny windows to the crude cabin I built. When my lamp was lit they shone out green in the night, those eyes to my green-eyed mansion."

"A green-eyed mansion on the ridge of Isle Royale," Greta said in a low tone. "Perhaps some day the whole world will learn of it and make a pilgrimage to it."

"God forbid!" said Percy O'Hara fervently.

CHAPTER TWENTY-EIGHT

TREASURE AT LAST

Vincent Stearns and Percy O'Hara bade their young friends farewell at dawn. With Swen they went gliding away toward Rock Harbor Lodge. They would wait the coming of a passing steamer that would carry them home.

When the chill damp of morning was gone, the three girls spread blankets, on the sand and fell fast asleep.

It was mid-afternoon when they sat down to the first meal of the day. It was a regal feast, for Swen had left two large, juicy steaks, and Vincent had contributed a large box of chocolates.

While they were in the midst of this banquet there came from the bay a piercing scream. It was followed by a most ludicrous laugh.

"That," exclaimed Jane, jumping up, "is old Dizzy, the dear, crazy old loon! He survived the storm."

She threw him a large piece of fresh meat. After swallowing it at a gulp, he let forth one more burst of laughter, then went splashing away.

"Do you know," she said as she resumed her place, "we've got a few days left here? I, for one, am through with mysteries. I'm all for having a hilarious good time—boating, swimming, fishing, hiking, and never a care!"

This program was carried out until quite suddenly out of a clear sky mystery once more caught them. Nor will any of them live to regret it.

It all came about because Jane suggested that they row out to the reef where the unlucky *Pilgrim* had gone aground.

To them the reef was a mournful sight. Nothing appeared above the placid surface of the water. A little way down on the jagged rocks were the boilers and engines of the *Pilgrim*.

"And look!" Jane exclaimed. "There are barrels down there. Three barrels. Not very far down either. Barrels of oil, Swen said they were. They must have been shaken out of the hull, like peas out of a pod. But barrels of oil. You'd think they might be worth something."

Then, like a flash, a thought came to her. "That man on the schooner, the diver, what was he after? Could it be—?" She dared not trust herself to think further. Swen was coming that night with supplies. She would tell him about the barrels. Perhaps he could tell them what to do about them.

"Yes," Swen agreed at once when he had been told of the discovery, "those barrels of oil are worth quite a little. Their worth depends on the kind of oil they hold. If it's linseed oil they'd be worth quite a goodly sum. Lubricating oil is cheaper, but would be worth going after. We could dive down and put on grappling hooks. Drag them up on the reef. That should not be very hard to do."

"Well!" Jane exclaimed. "We've been three last passengers and castaways. Now we are about to turn wreckers!"

And wreckers they were. They found it an easy task to attach the grappling irons to the barrels, then with a cable attached to Swen's small power boat to drag the first two barrels to the dry surface of the jagged reef.

The third barrel presented difficulties. It appeared unusually heavy. Twice the hooks slipped off. The third time the capstan on the boat gave way. But they did not give up their task easily. They were after the third barrel and meant to have it. In time this third barrel lay beside its two companions on the reef, well above water.

"There you are!" Swen exulted. "A fine day's work! We'll just tie up and have a look." He nosed the boat inshore and began the inspection of the barrels.

"Huh!" he grunted a short time later. "Two barrels of lubricating oil. Not so good.

"But look!" he explained. "What's this? This third barrel has rubbed against the rock until it got

"It's a Barrel of Gold!" Jane Cried

a hole in its side. No oil in that."

Just at that moment Jane caught sight of something that set her heart racing—a glint of gold from that hole in the barrel.

"Sw-wen!" she said shakily. "Just help me roll that barrel over."

"Why? What?" Swen complied, and as he did so a golden coin rolled from the hole that had been worn in the barrel.

"It's a barrel of gold!" Jane sat down suddenly. She sat in a puddle of water on the concave side of a rock and did not know it.

A barrel of gold it was—no less. The head of the steel barrel had been removed. A great number of gold coins, wrapped in paper, had been packed inside, then the head had been sealed up by steel welding. When the barrel had been painted, it looked just like any other.

Three hours later when the little fishing boat pulled away she carried a considerable treasure all in gold coins.

"Of course," Swen warned, "it's not our gold. But there's something in it for us all the same. Salvage, I guess you would call it."

The mystery of that barrel of gold was not solved at once. Little by little it became known that a very rich and stubborn man had refused to give up his hoarded gold when the United States Government, for the good of all its people, demanded that he should. Thinking to evade the law, he had packed his gold in a metal barrel and had attempted to ship it to Canada, and, as we know, had failed for on that trip the *Pilgrim* had been wrecked.

Just who the men were on the schooner, with the diver on board, will probably never be revealed. Were they hired by the rich man to retrieve the treasure? Were they plain thieves who, having got some knowledge of the gold, proposed to take it for themselves? No one ever found out just who they were.

Before the girls left the island a rumor was set afloat that there were bears to be found on the island. It was traced to the mainland. It was discovered there that a certain man of doubtful character had started the rumor. As proof of his story he displayed scratched hands and tattered clothing. He had met the bear, he said, by the old lighthouse at the end of Rock Harbor.

"That," Jeanne laughed, "must have been the head hunter. It was my bear he met. I'm glad, though," she added, "that he escaped with his life. The bear punished him quite enough."

The three girls were back in their city homes when the salvage on their barrel of gold arrived. Finding it to be quite a tidy sum, they promptly divided it in two parts and sent one part to Swen to be used for the best interests of his fisherfolk. That which remained they placed in the bank, a treasure hoard to be spent, in part at least, on some further adventure.